Kathryn Lamb lives in Dorset with her children. As well as writing books, she draws cartoons for *Private Eye*, *The Oldie*, *The Spectator* and *The Blackmore Vale Magazine*.

Also by Kathryn Lamb:

Eco-Worriers: *Penguin Problems*
Eco-Worriers: *Tree Trouble*
Eco-Worriers: *Saving the Bacon*
Best Mates Forever: *Vices and Virtues*
Is Anyone's Family As Mad As Mine?

Dolphin Disasters

Kathryn Lamb

Piccadilly Press • London

First published in Great Britain in 2009
by Piccadilly Press Ltd,
5 Castle Road, London NW1 8PR
www.piccadillypress.co.uk

A catalogue record for this book is available from the British Library

ISBN: 978 1 85340 998 1 (paperback)

1 3 5 7 9 10 8 6 4 2

Printed in the UK by CPI Bookmarque, Croydon, CR0 4TD
Cover design by Simon Davis
Cover illustration by Sue Hellard

Chapter One

'That is so unfair!' I exclaim, bristling with eco-indignation.

Mum has just told me that our neighbour, elderly Mrs Baggot, has moaned about finding a discarded plastic bottle in her front garden. She told Mum that she has noticed that young people on their way to school buy snacks and fizzy drinks from the corner shop and then drop the wrappers and empty plastic bottles in the street or throw them into people's gardens.

'What a cheek!' I explode. 'I have never done anything like that!'

'I don't think she specifically meant you, dear,' says Mum, soothingly. 'You know what Enid Baggot's like – her favourite hobby is complaining. But she has a point – I've noticed a lot of litter in the street, recently. Mrs Baggot said that litter is a national disgrace, and she thinks that parents and schools should be targeted in a campaign to clean up the area.'

'I still think it's unfair to blame it all on people on their way to school,' I say. 'It could be anyone – lots of people drop litter. But I agree that it's disgusting.'

'Mrs Baggot says that part of the problem is that young people don't eat a proper breakfast,' Mum continues. 'So they fill up on snacks and fizzy drinks on their way to school – hence the litter.'

'Ah! So it's definitely not me, then!' I say smugly, finishing my healthy nutritious breakfast of mini-wheats with half a sliced banana, followed by a slice of wholemeal toast with choconut spread, plus an additional spoonful of choconut spread for extra energy. This is important for Olympic hopefuls, such as myself. One of my New Year's resolutions was to step up my training schedule, cycling and swimming more, and running to and from school every day . . .

'Slow down!' gasps Evie, struggling to keep up with me. '*Pleeease* slow down!'

'But I've got to keep running,' I reply, over my shoulder. 'It was my New Year's resolution – remember?'

I am determined to keep my New Year's resolution as I am already feeling fitter – and I can do up my skinny jeans without experiencing breathing and sitting-down difficulties when they are on!

'But New Year was over a month ago!' Evie protests. 'Most normal people give up their New Year's resolutions halfway through January – they don't carry on well into February.'

'I've got will-power – unlike some people,' I yell at her, laughing and racing away before she can catch up with me to whack me with her bag. One of Evie's New Year's resolutions was to give up chocolate – this lasted until halfway through the afternoon on the first of January, when she devoured a whole bag of chocolate coins. Another of her New Year's resolutions was to be nice to everyone. She kept this one until the second of January, when she fell out with her brother Liam after she discovered that he'd eaten the rest of her Christmas chocolate, assuming – wrongly – that she no longer wanted it.

'Come on, Evie!' I call to her. 'Think about how fit you'll be after all this exercise!'

'I'm thinking about how dead I am going to be if you don't slow down!' Evie gasps. 'Oh – look!' She stops and stares up at the branches of a nearby tree, where a Kwikspend supermarket plastic bag is caught, rustling slightly in the breeze.

I stop and stare at it, angrily. As committed eco-worriers, Evie and I are both concerned about the number of plastic bags being thrown away and sent to landfill, causing plastic pollution, instead of being reused or recycled. I tell Evie about Mrs Baggot's complaint about litter being thrown into her front garden, as she gives me a boost up to grab the bag down. I put it in my schoolbag in case I need it some time. We agree that more needs to be done to persuade people to pick up litter and dispose of it properly, and we decide to redouble our eco-efforts, both at home and at school.

'Eco-worriers will triumph!' yells Evie. 'Together we will defeat the plastic menace!'

It is morning break on Monday and we are standing in the draughty courtyard, stamping our feet to keep warm. A sharp breeze whirls a couple of discarded cereal bar wrappers around our ankles.

'People still aren't getting the message!' exclaims Evie angrily, stooping to pick up the wrappers. 'Why are you all standing around knee-deep in rubbish? Why don't you do something about it – like pick it up?'

She isn't addressing anyone in particular, but Aisha takes her remarks personally.

'I'm always picking up rubbish!' she retorts. 'So stop having a go at me! I'm tired of your nagging!'

'Yes – stop making us all feel bad!' says Jack.

'I'm not!' Evie exclaims. 'I mean – that's not what I want to do. I just want everyone to help get rid of all the litter responsibly, and use the recycling bins when they can, otherwise what's the point of having them?'

Jack pretends to nod off, snoring loudly. Evie glares at him.

'Perhaps we could have a litter-pick,' I suggest, wanting to support Evie, but not wanting to nag. 'It needn't be too difficult. Just stuff any litter in your pockets or your schoolbags until you get to the bins – the recycling ones if it's the right sort of litter.'

'Yuk!' exclaims Shaheen. 'I don't want other people's putrid rubbish in my pockets, or my bag!'

'Eww!' says Amelia, who has joined us with her retinue of So Cool Girls, as we call them. 'You can forget it! I'm certainly not doing *that*! Think of all the *germs*!' Amelia flutters her hands in front of her face as if feeling faint. 'Trust you to have such a rubbish idea!' she scoffs at us.

All the So Cool Girls go 'EWW!' in unison.

'You're rubbish, Amelia!' Evie snaps back. 'Why don't you go and recycle yourself and come back as someone nicer?'

'Speak for yourself, eco-freak!' Amelia snaps back.

Amelia and the So Cool Girls melt away, sneering at us over their shoulders. Evie and I turn our backs on them.

'OK,' I continue. 'As I was saying, before that rude interruption, I don't mind how we do it – we could bring in a bin-liner tomorrow, perhaps —'

'A recycled one, of course,' interrupts Evie.

'Yes – a recycled one – and you could use it to put litter in.' I look at everyone hopefully, and smile brightly in what I hope is a winning way.

There is a distinct lack of response.

'Why are Ellen, Gemma, Victoria and Danii standing over there, whispering and giving you funny looks?' Lee asks Evie.

'I've no idea,' replies Evie, shortly. Her arms are still tightly folded.

I look warily over to where Ellen, Gemma, Victoria and Danii are standing. I give them a little wave, but they don't wave back. They are joined by Cassia and Salma, and they immediately start whispering to them and giving Evie – and me – more strange looks.

'I've a good mind to go and ask them what their problem is!' Evie mutters to me angrily. 'Why are they being so weird?' she asks the people around us – but the conversation has jumped to the more exciting subject of next week's school trip to a sea life centre. Evie and I are thrilled to be going there and everyone else is equally excited – although Jack and Lee are mainly excited at the thought of getting out of lessons for a day. We join in the happy chatter – but it is a shame that we couldn't whip up a similar amount of enthusiasm for picking up litter.

I feel discouraged during double maths. It is not unusual for me to feel discouraged during double maths, but today I feel especially discouraged because of our friends' bad reaction to the litter-pick idea, and the 'green fatigue' which seems to have swept through the school recently – no one is that bothered about being green.

Evie and I even had to give up our healthy eating stall due to lack of support. People's interest in it tailed off and we found that we were spending more on ingredients than we were making from the stall.

I have also noticed that people's eyes tend to glaze over whenever Evie or I mention 'saving the world'.

Jack's reaction when Evie was talking about recycling – pretending to go to sleep – has become alarmingly common.

I am not sure what Evie or I can do about it, and I must be looking worried because Mr Hobson, the maths teacher, approaches me and says, gently, 'I know that you find equations challenging, Evie – but please don't get upset! Let me help you.'

The next lesson after double maths is geography. Before the lesson begins, Evie and I go up to Mr Woodsage at the front of the class and, over the background noise of chatter and the scraping of chairs, we ask him if he will help us to get people properly organised to pick up the litter in the school grounds. He says that it is a great idea, and he will certainly give it some thought and get back to us.

As we return to our seats, Amelia hisses at us, 'Teacher's pets!'. We ignore her.

The lesson begins. We are learning about the plastic vortex in the Pacific Ocean. This is a huge swirling mass of plastic rubbish that has collected in the middle of the ocean, and consists mainly of plastic bags and plastic bottles. I can't help feeling sad about it – those things are so easy to reuse and recycle, but because people can't be bothered, it is spoiling the ocean instead, killing the sea creatures that live there. Hopefully this will inspire people to get involved in the litter-pick. Mr Woodsage tells us lots of fascinating facts, such as describing what happens when the plastic reaches land.

'It's like a big animal,' he says. 'It moves around and, when it reaches land, it vomits, and you get a beach covered in plastic rubbish.'

'Eurgh!' exclaims Aisha. 'That's disgusting!'

The lesson continues. Amelia gets told off for whispering. Jemima gets told off for whispering. Jack gets told off for whispering. Even Shaheen, who never misbehaves, gets told off for whispering.

I look around uneasily. What is going on? Why are they all whispering? I notice that Ellen is glaring at me, and Cassia is giving Evie a hard stare. Evie is staring back, mouthing, '*What?*'.

I catch Amelia's eye, and a big sly grin slides across her face.

'Could you all please concentrate on your work?' Mr Woodsage appeals to the class, taking off his little round glasses and cleaning them. He has short, stubbly hair and a short neatly-trimmed beard, and he is the most eco-minded of all the teachers. He is very popular and doesn't usually have any trouble with bad behaviour during his lessons.

As we leave the classroom at the end of the lesson, Ellen pushes past me roughly.

'Watch out, Ellen!' I exclaim. 'You nearly knocked me over!'

'It's no more than you deserve!' she snaps at me.

'What? What are you talking about?' Evie and I demand, following her and Cassia down the corridor. 'Can someone please tell us what's going on?'

'You *know*!' retorts Ellen, spinning around and confronting us.

'Know what?' I appeal to her.

'You and Evie want Mr Woodsage to give us extra homework. You want him to give us special eco-homework. You're so keen to stuff your pick-up-a-plastic-wrapper-and-save-the-world campaign down our throats that you want him to hand out eco-detentions if we don't do our eco-homework well enough! And we're all going to get eco-detentions if we don't pick up all the litter in the school! I wouldn't mind helping you if you didn't keep trying to force people to be green – and now you're getting a teacher to make sure we all do it.'

'But that's rubbish – literally!' I exclaim.

'Who told you all this?' Evie asks.

'Amelia.'

'And you believed her?' Evie is incensed.

'But you know what Amelia's like!' I appeal to Ellen. 'She's always starting rumours and stirring things!'

'I can't believe that you took her seriously,' says Evie, running her hands through her red curls in frustration. 'And now you've told other people, and they believed you?'

'They believe that you'll do anything to get people picking up litter and doing what you want them to do. And they think you're sucking up to Mr Woodsage because he supports the same green causes as you do.'

'We do *not* suck up to Mr Woodsage!' explodes Evie. 'All we did was ask for his help organising a litter-pick! I would *never* ask for extra homework. What kind of an idiot do you think I am? And no one's getting any eco-detentions, so you really needn't worry.'

'You make us sound like eco-bullies,' I say in a low voice, feeling very hurt.

'You do tend to go on about litter and recycling and stuff,' remarks Lee, who is walking down the corridor beside us. 'And on. And on . . .'

'Well – I'm *sorry*!' exclaims Evie, her face flushing an angry red under her freckles. 'I'm so sorry for caring about the world we live in!' And she rushes off to the girls' cloakroom in tears. I go after her.

Unfortunately, Amelia and a crowd of So Cool Girls are in the cloakroom.

'Oh dear!' drawls Amelia. 'What's wrong with you, Evie? You've gone all red. Are you suffering from global warming?'

The So Cool Girls titter and flock around Amelia.

'Leave Evie alone!' I shout at Amelia. 'And stop spreading stupid rumours, Amelia – it's pathetic!'

'*You're* pathetic!' Amelia retorts. 'Haven't you noticed? No one likes you!'

'Let's go somewhere else,' I mutter to Evie, grabbing her arm and dragging her out of the cloakroom before she has a chance to explode at Amelia. I can feel her seething.

We sit outside in the courtyard to eat our lunch, perched on the circular seat around our favourite tree. But all the flavour seems to have gone out of my tub of sun-dried tomato pasta with pesto and roasted pine nuts. Evie seems to have lost her appetite, too. No one comes to join us, or talk to us.

'Do we smell, or something?' Evie asks.

'I suppose Amelia's stupid rumours have had an effect,' I say, 'even if people are beginning to find out they're not true.'

'I hate it when people talk behind your back!' Evie exclaims. She doesn't seem willing to accept any responsibility for upsetting people, although I can understand how our repeated attempts to spread the eco-message may be getting on people's nerves. Perhaps we need to talk about other things for a while, such as music, clothes, school trips and so on. But I am unwilling to upset Evie further by mentioning this. Maybe I will have a word later about broadening her topics of conversation.

A thin cold drizzle begins to fall. Evie picks up a couple of empty plastic bottles, and I go with her to take them to the recycling bins.

Eco-info

13 billion plastic bottles are thrown away in the UK each year that could have been recycled, or, better still, reused. Many products can be made from recycled plastic - from new plastic bottles, to bin-liners and even fleece jackets!

Chapter Two

I am very relieved when the school day comes to an end. I put on my trainers – I am looking forward to running home in order to relieve some of the stress which I have felt building up inside me during what has been an awful day.

'Slow down! *Pleeease!*' Evie calls to me, as she struggles to keep up. I know that I am running faster than usual. But I am in no mood to slow my pace, until I nearly trip and fall over Boris the cat on the corner of Frog Street.

'Come . . . back . . . to . . . my . . . house!' Evie pants. 'Please! I . . . need . . . company!'

Upstairs in her room, Evie collapses in a mock fainting fit on her bed.

I feel all wobbly and trembly from exertion, which makes me think that I am not yet fit enough for the Olympics. I must do some extra training! But I am not quite as quivering and jellified as Evie, who asks me in a faint voice to go and fetch her some apple juice.

'Why do I have to go and get it?' I ask.

'You nearly killed me – it's the least you can do!' she bleats.

'You didn't *have* to try and keep up with me!' I point out. But I am thirsty too, so I fetch us some drinks from the kitchen. There seems to be no one else around.

'Thanks,' says Evie gratefully, when I return with the drinks. 'Sometimes I wish you weren't such an exercise freak, Lola. You're always charging up and down the hockey field, billowing clouds of steam, or dashing madly to and fro across the netball court. That's when you're not cycling or swimming or jogging or doing sit-ups or —'

'OK, OK! Just wait till I win a gold medal in the next Olympics!' I reply, smiling.

'That's the first time I've seen you smile today,' Evie observes.

'It hasn't been a smiling sort of day, has it?' I say. 'You haven't exactly split your sides laughing, either.'

'It felt like everyone was turning against us. It was horrible. I really don't think we deserve it – do you?'

'Er – not really, but . . .' I am about to point out as gently as possible that no one likes being nagged, when Evie, who has wandered over to her bedroom window, calls me over. She points down at the street below.

'What can you see?' she asks.

'Frog Street. Daffodils. Hedges. A cat. A man walking past.'

'What else? Look!' Evie points at something in the street, jabbing her finger agitatedly.

'Er . . . oh! There's a plastic bag blowing down the street.'

'Yes!'

'And there's another one caught on that hedge over there. And there's an empty plastic bottle in the road. And a crisp packet in next door's garden – someone must have chucked it over the hedge, like Mrs Baggot said . . .'

'So let's go and pick it up!' exclaims Evie, enthusiastically. 'Let's tackle plastic pollution head-on!'

'OK – but I don't really fancy picking up other people's rubbish.'

'We can wear rubber gloves – Mum's got some in

17

the kitchen. We can wash them when we've finished. Come on – let's go litter-picking!'

Half an hour later, armed with two black bin-liners – one for litter that can be recycled and one for litter that can't – and wearing one pink floral rubber glove each – Evie's mum is at work and we could only find one pair of gloves – Evie and I have lost some of our initial enthusiasm. It is cold outside and the wind is blowing our hair around.

'Ewww!' splutters Evie, gingerly pulling a wet, muddy plastic bag out from under a hedge on the corner of Frog Street and Newton Close, and dropping it into her bin-liner. 'This is gross!'

'It was your idea,' I remind her. I have half filled my bin-liner, mostly with discarded Kwikspend plastic carrier bags, which we will take to be recycled at the supermarket, although we may have to hose them down first! We have also picked up crisp and sweet wrappers and three or four empty plastic bottles.

'Eurgh! What's *that*?'

Evie extracts a greyish pink round blobby thing from under the hedge. Then she squeals, drops it and jumps back.

'Oh – yuk! Lola – what is it?'

'Er . . . it's a doll's head – minus the body. Someone's got a headless doll.'

'It's creepy!'

'It's staring at us.'

'We should pick it up.'

'Hello?' says a voice just behind us.

'AAARGH!!!' Evie and I both jump violently, spinning round to see our friend Ellen, who lives in Newton Close, looking at us curiously.

'What are you doing?' she asks. She seems friendlier now than she was at school. Perhaps she has realised that Amelia was spreading nasty rumours about us and we are not that bad, really!

'Ohmigod! You gave me such a shock!' Evie exclaims, recovering her breath and her composure. 'You shouldn't creep up on people like that!'

'Sorry!' says Ellen. 'Why are you wearing a pink glove and carrying a bin-liner?'

I explain that we don't just want to clear litter at school – we want to rid our neighbourhood of it, too. I ask her if she'd like to help.

Ellen wrinkles her nose and backs away slightly. 'I'm . . . not sure . . .' she says, uncertainly.

'But think about the animals which are choking to

death on dropped litter!' exclaims Evie, a little over-dramatically. Ellen looks around, as if expecting choking birds and squirrels to drop out of the trees, and rabbits and badgers and other creatures to stumble out of the bushes, all tangled up in plastic. 'Do you want that on your conscience? Because we're all to blame unless we do something to help!'

'And it just looks so awful!' I add, hastily, as Evie seems to be driving the eco-message home too forcefully again, and Ellen is backing away.

'We've picked up so many Kwikspend bags,' I add. 'That supermarket should stop handing out so many plastic bags – it's a nightmare!'

'We should stage a protest,' Evie suggests. 'We could stand outside Kwikspend and tell people not to use new plastic bags for their shopping. It's easy enough to take old ones or, better still, switch to a reusable carrier, made of jute or organic cotton – or take a pull-along shopping trolley.'

Ellen wrinkles her nose up at this last idea.

Evie continues, oblivious and clearly on a roll. 'Even Mum's done that. In fact, she sells organic cotton bags in her shop. But when she's in a hurry, she sometimes forgets and uses plastic bags for convenience.'

Ellen is now looking slightly dazed. 'I only came

out for some fresh air,' she says, weakly. 'I might go in again. It's nearly time for *Sunset Road*.'

'Oh! Is it that time already?' Evie exclaims.

'Time flies when you're having as much fun as we've been having!' I remark, dryly.

Sunset Road is our favourite Australian soap, and nearly everyone in our Year watches it, especially the girls.

'Craig from Boys Next Door is making a special guest appearance today,' says Ellen. 'As a lifeguard.'

'Oh – *wow!*' Evie and I exchange glances. Surely picking up litter can wait for twenty-five minutes?

'We'll carry on with this later,' says Evie firmly, reading my mind. 'Come and watch *Sunset Road* with us, Ellen. Let's hurry, it's about to start!'

We rush back to Evie's house, leaving our bin-liners and floral gloves on the lawn outside the house, and soon we are all huddled up together on the sofa, transfixed by *Sunset Road* and squealing our appreciation when Craig from Boys Next Door makes his appearance. Evie's brother, Liam, enters the room briefly, looks at us and at the television, and leaves again in disgust.

Seeing Liam, however briefly, always makes my insides do a back flip! I love the way his dark floppy fringe falls across his dark brown eyes.

I am vaguely aware, while the programme is on, that the wind outside has got stronger, and I can hear fences creaking, gates rattling, and the sound of something, possibly someone's wheelie bin, tipping over. The wind howls around the house and I'm glad we're indoors watching Craig from Boys Next Door.

As *Sunset Road* finishes, we hear the crunching of a car's tyres on the gravel drive. Evie's dad collects her mum from her shop, Fashion Passion, and brings her home at about this time each day.

But today there are different sounds outside, apart from the slamming of car doors. We hear angry voices shouting.

'What on earth's going on?' Evie asks, as we all twist round on the sofa and look through the window to see who is shouting.

Evie's dad bursts into the room. 'Evie! There you are! What have you been doing? There's a terrible mess outside!'

'Mess? But we've been picking up litter.'

'Well I'm sorry, but it looks as if you've been throwing it around. You'd better come out and explain. Mrs Baggot's not happy at all.'

With a sense of foreboding, I troop outside after

Evie and her dad, closely followed by Ellen, who looks genuinely scared.

I hear Evie's sharp intake of breath and her muttered exclamation of 'Oh *no!*' – and then I see why.

The wind, which has now dropped to the occasional cold gust, has obviously blown the contents of our bin bags all over the street. My heart sinks as I realise that, because we were rushing to catch the beginning of *Sunset Road*, we must have forgotten to tie up the bin bags. Even more unfortunately, a lot of the rubbish has ended up in Mrs Baggot's front garden, which is opposite Evie's house.

'Ah! The culprits!' exclaims Mrs Baggot in a nasty voice. She shakes a knobbly finger at us, like a witch. Her windswept grey hair adds to the effect, and I find myself moving a little behind Evie.

'She means us, doesn't she?' whispers Ellen, edging behind me.

'Don't worry,' I whisper back. 'I'll tell her you had nothing to do with it.'

'Oh no! Oh no!' Evie exclaims, cupping her hands to her face. 'This is a disaster!'

'It's a disaster for *me!*' shrieks the irate Mrs Baggot, increasingly witchlike – all she needs is a broom. 'What on earth possessed you to throw all that litter into our gardens?'

'We were trying to clear it up and then the wind must have blown it around again!' Evie gabbles desperately. But her mum and dad and Mrs Baggot are still looking cross. With a sinking sensation I see my mum and dad coming up the road to see what is going on. Even Liam is standing in the doorway behind us, arms folded, grinning.

'It's not funny,' Evie hisses at him furiously.

'Uh-oh! Sense of humour failure!' Liam remarks unhelpfully.

'Shut up, Liam!' Evie hisses through clenched teeth.

'We were only trying to help,' I say, imploringly.

Ellen says that she has to go home for her tea and edges away.

Evie's dad takes charge. 'Evie, Lola – I'd like you both to apologise to Mrs Baggot.' Mum and Dad nod their agreement with this.

Evie looks stubborn, but I am keen to defuse the whole silly situation.

'Sorry, Mrs Baggot,' I say.

'Evie?'

'ErmsorryMrsBaggot,' Evie mutters.

'It sounds like the girls had good intentions,' says Evie's dad.

Oh! At last! Sanity prevails! Evie's dad is *cool*.

'But they should obviously have disposed of the rubbish more carefully,' Evie's dad continues. 'They'll clear up all the mess immediately, won't you, girls?'

We both nod gloomily. Not *again*!

'And thanks for ruining my only pair of decent rubber gloves!' says Evie's mum, crossly.

It takes us another half hour to pick up all the scattered litter to Mrs Baggot's satisfaction. She stands in her doorway, wrapped in a thick brown shawl, and tells us not to tread on any of her plants.

'I'm fed up with young people throwing litter into my garden!' she squawks shrilly.

I sense Evie bridling at this and quickly put a calming hand on her arm.

'I don't think she realises we're trying to help,' I whisper. 'It's probably best not to say anything – she's not in the best of moods.'

'She's not the only one!' Evie mutters under her breath.

I go home for my tea – parsnip soufflé, which is my particular favourite.

Feeling the need to escape, I ask if I can go back to

Evie's house for a while. I want to check that she is OK.

I find Evie lying on her bed, looking totally exhausted.

'Are you OK?' I ask.

'I don't know. Are you?'

'Sort of.'

'I still want to stop plastic pollution. Remember how Mr Woodsage told us about it clogging up the ocean and choking dolphins and turtles and other sea creatures – as well as land creatures? I forgot to mention that to Ellen.'

'Perhaps we'd better leave Ellen alone for a while, after today. She looked quite stressed by the argument with Mrs Baggot, let alone the litter-pick. But we needn't give up.'

'Certainly not!' exclaims Evie, reviving. 'Eco-worriers never give up. We've just suffered a setback.'

'That's right. A temporary setback,' I agree.

'At least we managed to put most of that rubbish in the recycling bin – eventually.'

'Yes. Although your mum didn't seem too happy to find her recycling bin stuffed with other people's rubbish.'

'No . . . I expect she's tired, that's all.'

'Like we are.'

Evie yawns loudly. 'I'm beginning to feel better,' she says. 'I'm glad you're here, Lola. Let's plan our plastic bag protest.'

'Oh – are you serious about that?'

'Of course! Ellen said she'd join us, didn't she?'

'Er . . . I still think we should leave Ellen alone for a while,' I reply.

'I don't see why,' Evie says. 'Let's email her. Let's email all our friends and arrange to meet outside Kwikspend on Saturday morning! Not too early, because I need my beauty sleep, especially after a stressful week at school. Let's ask everyone to be there at twelve.'

'*Everyone?*' I ask. 'Isn't it rather short notice to organise a protest?' I realise that I have never organised a protest, either at short or long notice.

I don't think Evie has, either. But she is full of enthusiasm, exclaiming, 'It's never too soon to wage war on waste! We can start by not wasting time!'

Evie sits at her computer and writes an email to all our friends, telling them to be outside Kwikspend on Saturday at twelve. She tells them that we need to do something about rubbish in our streets and that the easiest way to do this is to stop the plastic bag menace.

So the protest will be about asking people to stop using new plastic bags.

'There!' she says, in a satisfied voice, pressing *Send*. 'That should do it. Why are you looking like a dying duck?'

'I'm not! I don't look anything like a dying duck!'

'Sorry! It's just something that Liam's always saying to me. But you look doubtful.'

'I'm doubtful whether our parents are going to be wildly supportive of us staging a protest, especially after today.'

'At least I'm taking positive action! And it's going to be a peaceful protest.'

'I should hope so!' I exclaim. 'Shall we listen to some music? It's a good way to relax.' I'm feeling a deep need to relax – I think I've had enough positive action for one day! I sit on Evie's bed, watching Posh and Pout the goldfish swimming round and round in their tank on her bedside table. Watching fish is supposed to be relaxing, too.

'*SHAKE SHAKE YOUR GREEN THING!*'

I nearly jump out of my skin. Evie is playing Greenrock's new single very loudly through her iPod speakers.

There is a sudden loud knocking on the bedroom

door and Liam bursts into the room.

'Can you turn that racket down?' he shouts. 'I'm trying to study, and you know I can't stand Greenrock. Their claim to be greener than green is rubbish and so is their music!'

'I didn't know you were here,' says Evie, turning the volume down.

'I was in my room.'

Evie peers out of her bedroom door across the landing to Liam's room.

'Why have you got all your lights on?' she asks. 'It's a waste of electricity. And you haven't even got energy-saving light bulbs in your room. This family needs to think a bit harder about its carbon footprint. I noticed that you boiled a whole kettle full of water this morning, just to make one cup of coffee. All you needed was a cup's worth of water. Kettles guzzle energy! And you're always leaving your mobile charger switched on all day. And —'

'STOP!' Liam shouts at her. 'Please – shut up! I didn't come in here for a lecture! Don't you realise how boring you're being, Evie, when you go on and on at people? I predict that long before we all perish because of raised sea levels, we are fated to die of boredom listening to eco-alarmists like you!'

I pretend to be totally fascinated by Posh and Pout as I don't want to be drawn into another argument between Liam and Evie. But Liam has already gone, slamming the door behind him, leaving his sister looking half angry, half shocked.

'How dare he!' she splutters. 'The cheek of it!'

I sigh heavily. 'Evie,' I say.

'Yes?'

'Er . . . do you think . . . maybe . . . Liam may be right? Or, at least, partly right?'

'What do you mean? Are you having a go at me as well, Lola?'

'No. No – of course not, Evie.'

'It's not fair!' Evie wails. 'Everyone's turning against me. The whole world's turning against me.And you're meant to be my best friend, Lola. My fellow eco-worrier!'

'I *am*! All I was trying to say was —'

'I don't care what you were trying to say. You've said enough!'

There is an awkward silence, broken only by Greenrock playing quietly:

'*Green is cool, it's cool to be green*
Let's go green together
Know what I mean?'

I don't know why Liam can't stand Greenrock, although I have to admit that their lyrics are a bit naff. Perhaps he is jealous of their success, even though he doesn't need to be because his own band, the Rock Hyraxes, are doing really well and have played several gigs recently.

Evie is sitting at the other end of her bed with her back to me, staring out of the window at the leaden sky. I continue to feign interest in Posh and Pout. They really aren't very interesting. My heart is beating fast because I find falling out with Evie very stressful. I didn't mean to upset her. I wonder which of us is going to speak first. In the event, we both start talking at once:

'I'm really sorry, Evie!'

'So what were you trying to say?' Evie asks.

We turn to look at each other.

'OK,' I say, 'before I say anything else, I just want to say that you're my best friend and I don't want anything to come between us – so *pleeease* can we not fall out?'

'OK,' says Evie. 'I agree. So what did you want to say before you said what you just said?'

'Er . . . I've forgotten. Oh, I remember! I think Greenrock summed it up just now when they were singing "*Green is cool, it's cool to be green*".'

Evie looks puzzled. 'I know it is,' she says.

'Yes, but we haven't made being green seem very cool when we're with anyone else. I don't think we've made it seem like much fun, just a lot of hard work. And . . . perhaps we've been putting people down more than we have been encouraging them? That doesn't help people want to change. I think that might be why people have been saying that we're boring – they don't like being lectured. I think that's why Liam flipped just now. Don't worry, I'm not accusing you! I'm just as bad. I upset Dad by nagging him and I think I've probably done the same thing to Mum.'

'I know what you mean. Mum told me off for nagging the other day.' She looks guilty for a moment. 'It wasn't the first time, either.'

'So maybe we need a different approach. We've got to make it fun to be green.'

'How?' Evie asks.

'We could start by talking to people about other stuff, apart from green issues. I don't want it to seem like we're totally obsessed with eco-this and eco-that.'

'You're right,' Evie agrees. 'I don't want to fall out with people – I like having a laugh with our friends and I enjoy a good gossip.'

'Well, not recently,' I point out, hesitantly.

'Oh,' says Evie, looking crestfallen. 'I'd better remind people that I'm still human. I need to be friendly as well as eco-friendly.'

'We should probably try the same approach with our families,' I suggest.

Evie nods. 'Thanks, Lola. I don't think I realised what I was doing . . . sorry if I've been a bit unbearable recently.'

'Oh, don't worry about it! I understand how you're feeling. I want to save the world as much as you do and it's really frustrating when people can't be bothered to do anything. What we need is a really fun idea to get people doing something for the environment.'

Evie sneezes. 'I think I'm getting a cold,' she says.

'Oh dear, try not to give it to me! It wouldn't be good for my Olympic training.'

'Thanks for the sympathy, Lola!'

Evie turns back to her computer. 'I just hope that people think that the protest outside Kwikspend is a fun idea,' she says.

'Hmm,' I say, doubtfully.

I am exhausted. Back in my own room, I lie in bed

gazing at the luminous stars on my bedroom ceiling, waiting for sleep to overtake me. I feel apprehensive about Saturday's planned peaceful protest. Will we get into a lot of trouble? It was bad enough today, just picking up litter! I wonder how many of our friends will turn up. Evie seems to be expecting a huge turnout and massive support for our anti-plastic-bag cause, but I am not so sure. There were no replies to Evie's rallying email when I left her house earlier this evening, apart from one from Aisha, saying she couldn't make it, and another one from Jack, telling us that Saturdays are for sleeping. Evie was disgusted by this. 'Not *all* day, surely!' she exclaimed.

My eyelids are heavy. The one happy thought in my head is of the visit to the sea life centre next Monday. I can't wait!

Eco-info

Every plastic bag handed out at tills is used, on average, for only 20 minutes before being discarded. Try to only use a new bag when you really need it. Keep a spare used plastic bag, or another bag that can be rolled up, in your main schoolbag or handbag. It will mean you don't have to ask for a new one in the shops.

Chapter Three

I *usually sleep in* on Saturday mornings, but for some reason, most probably anxiety about Evie's plans to go protesting outside Kwikspend today – Oh no! *Today!* – I wake up early and can't go back to sleep. So I get up and go for a bike ride, taking my binoculars with me in case I spot any unusual birds – bird-watching has been a hobby of mine for as long as I can remember.

I love cycling too, because I feel free and love the feeling of the wind against my face. Cycling is also part of my bid to get as fit as possible in order to try out for the next Olympics *and* it's eco-friendly! I believe strongly in pedal power and I like to think that I am pedalling my way to a better future.

It is a beautiful cold, crisp, sunny morning, and

there is an almost spring-like feeling. The birds seem to feel it too and they are singing more loudly. I stop to admire a pair of pied wagtails, hopping and darting around in the street outside my house, before putting my bike away. I am ready for my miniwheats and choconut spread.

'What are you doing today?' Mum asks as she makes a cup of tea.

'Oh, I'll probably go round to Evie's,' I reply, innocently. 'We're going to Kwikspend with her parents and we might meet up with some friends.'

I decide not to mention the peaceful protest. I don't want to worry her or stress her out.

When I arrive in Evie's room, she has a banner spread out on the floor, with the slogan *Make Plastic Bags History* written on it in large green letters.

'It looks good, doesn't it?' she says, happily.

'Ye-e-e-s,' I hesitate. 'But aren't we persuading people to reuse and recycle plastic bags, as well as making them history?'

'You try putting all of that on one banner!' Evie retorts, grumpily. 'I wanted to write something snappy, to get people's attention.'

'OK,' I say. 'The banner's fine. But are we really

going to stand outside Kwikspend with it? Won't we look a bit stupid?'

'There's nothing stupid about saving the world, Lola!' she says, sternly. Then she relaxes, and giggles. 'I don't care – it'll be a laugh! All our friends will be there.'

I wish I shared her confidence about this. I haven't detected a great deal of enthusiasm for the planned protest in any of our friends over the past few days, although a few of them, under intense pressure from Evie, have rather grudgingly said that they will make it there. Jack is still insisting that he needs his beauty sleep. But Evie has been making strenuous efforts not to lose her temper and to be friendly, and talk to people about other things apart from green issues. People do seem to be relieved about this.

'I like your hair!' she says to me, as if proving the point.

'Thanks.' I have made two little plaits, tied up with red and green bands. I am wearing my skinny red jeans, and I hope I don't look too tired. I want to look good, in case I see Liam. I think that Liam is cool, but I don't want Evie to know that I fancy him, because that would be totally embarrassing. So I keep the gooey feelings in my stomach to myself whenever he is around.

Evie insists on waving the banner around, holding it above her head, as we walk to Kwikspend. It is a bright clear day – 'Good protesting weather!' Evie remarks – and a cool light breeze is blowing. 'If we make just one person think twice about using new bags or just binning their plastic bags, it will be worth it!' says Evie, confidently.

'Did you tell your parents what you're doing?' I ask. I feel strangely guilty about not having told Mum and Dad, although at least they know where I am. But what if I get arrested? It will be a terrible shock for them. I remember watching a news programme which showed policemen on horseback breaking up protests, and using riot shields, and suddenly feel queasy.

'I told Dad I was doing a school project about plastic bags,' Evie replies, breezily. 'I told him I needed to interview the manager of Kwikspend. Parents will agree to almost anything if you tell them it's for a school project – or that it's going to save them money,' she declares.

I wonder if we will meet the manager of Kwikspend. I hope he isn't scary. I have a feeling that

Evie exercising her right to stage a peaceful protest against plastic bags might not bring out the best in him.

I can't see any of our friends outside Kwikspend, although there are crowds of shoppers. We wait ten minutes – but no one turns up. We give it another five. Reluctantly, we realise that we *are* the protest.

We stand just outside the entrance. Evie looks slightly less confident now. She nudges me and hisses at me to take one end of the banner so that we can hold it out between us. Most of the shoppers pass by without giving us a second glance, although a few stare at the banner and then at us. I feel acutely self-conscious and embarrassed. I wish some of our friends would turn up, although I am not surprised that they haven't. They obviously don't want to feel like I do.

'Evie,' I whisper, 'how stupid do you think we look, on a scale of one to ten?'

'Eight,' Evie replies. 'And a half. I'm really disappointed that no one's turned up to support us.'

'Shall we just go?'

'No! Not yet!'

'Evie?'

'What?'

'There's a man staring at us. He won't stop staring. Don't look now – he's just inside the entrance. Oh! He's coming towards us!'

'Lola! Just calm down! You keep jiggling about – hold the banner still!'

A man in a smart black suit, with slicked-down dark hair and a neat side-parting, is now standing directly in front of us.

'We do sell reusable fabric shopping bags, you know,' he says. 'We don't make the customers use plastic bags. We offer them the choice.'

He gives us a long, hard look. 'I'm the manager of this store,' he says. I see that his name badge says *Keith Norris*. 'Don't you think you should have asked my permission before staging a protest outside the entrance?'

'Oh . . . er . . . we're really sorry!' we both stammer.

The manager seems to relent. He smiles. 'You obviously care about the environment,' he says. 'So do I. But I also have a business to run. So I'd be grateful if you'd roll up your banner now. You're welcome to shop in the store if you wish, as long as you don't accost any of my customers, or bother them in any way.'

I am mortified. I realise he's only being kind

because he sees how feeble the protest is and feels sorry for us.

'Oh, we won't!' I exclaim. He smiles at us in a half-hearted sort of way and goes back inside the store. I have no desire to accost or bother anyone. I want to roll up the banner and run away! To make matters worse, the whole encounter with the Kwikspend manager has been witnessed by Amelia, who has just arrived with her parents to do the shopping and has stopped to sneer at us.

Amelia's dad is short and round, with thinning hair combed over his balding head. Her mum, who works as a freelance journalist under the name of Rhona Tweeks, is tall and willowy, like her daughter, with long dyed blond curls, bright red lipstick and heavy make-up, and she teeters along on bright red high heels, towering over her husband. They go on into the store while Amelia hangs back a few paces behind them, looking sulky.

'It's not exactly cool behaviour to go shopping with your parents, is it?' says Evie in an extra-loud whisper which she obviously intends Amelia to overhear.

Amelia glares at us sourly. 'What are you doing?' she asks, abruptly. 'Isn't it a bit weird, standing outside Kwikspend with a stupid piece of paper?' She peers at our banner and curls her top lip contemptuously. 'Oh, I forgot. You *are* weird! That manager certainly thought you were.'

'At least we're doing something to help the world,' I snap back. 'Plastic bags are polluting the land and the sea. Don't you care?'

Amelia tosses back her long blond hair. 'Whatever,' she says.

'Your dad's factory still makes plastic, doesn't it?' says Evie, accusingly.

Amelia yawns loudly. 'I don't know. He's changed the name of his business from Plunkett's Plastics to Plunkett's Recyclable Materials. There! Are you happy now?'

'It's just a name. I hope he really *does* use recyclable or recycled materials. I know that you *can* get recyclable plastic – but people still throw it away in normal bins and it still ends up going to landfill. And what about all the packaging? Modern packaging has left Britain drowning in a sea of plastic waste!'

Amelia yawns again. 'You really are *boring*,' she says. 'No wonder you don't have any friends.'

Evie looks uncomfortable.

'You'd better run along and catch up with your parents, Amelia,' I say. 'Do you go shopping in

Kwikspend a lot? I thought designer shops were more your style.'

Amelia throws a final withering look back over her shoulder at us as she disappears into Kwikspend, which is filling up with more and more customers.

'Where *are* all our friends?' Evie wonders anxiously. 'It's a bit bad that none of them could be bothered to turn up.'

I feel disappointed, too. 'It would have been nice to have some support,' I comment.

'You have my support!' booms a familiar voice. It belongs to our friend Meltonio, the eco-friendly ice-cream seller, who has come shopping with his wife and brood of mini-Meltonios.

'I was in the store doing my weekly shop and buying things for Luigi, too, for his restaurant.' Luigi is Meltonio's brother and Meltonio works in Luigi's restaurant, Samson's, when he is not selling ice-cream. 'And then I saw you standing outside with your banner,' Meltonio continues. 'I was going to come and join you, but then I saw the manager having words with you. It is a shame. I think it is a good thing to see young people standing up for what they believe in. Especially when it is such an important thing. I agree with you that plastic bags are very

45

bad – they are polluting our beautiful world. At least I have brought some nice big reusable carriers with me today – otherwise you would make me feel ashamed!'

At last! We have a supporter!

'Thanks, Meltonio!' we both say. We ask after Samson the pig, who was saved from slaughter after we persuaded Meltonio not to eat him for Christmas but to keep him alive and breed from him instead. Meltonio replies that Samson and Samson's wife, Delilah, are both well, and announces proudly that they are expecting the pitter-patter of tiny trotters very soon.

'Oh, how exciting!' Evie exclaims, her eyes shining. 'Can we come and visit them as soon as they're born, Meltonio?'

'Of course! Of course!'

After Meltonio has gone, Evie looks serious again. 'We've really got to think of other ways to get the message about the harmful effects of plastic bag pollution across,' says Evie. 'People keep coming out of Kwikspend with loads of plastic bags – look!'

This is true. People emerge from the store trundling trolleys piled high with enough shopping to sink a battleship – and it is mostly in fresh plastic bags.

Despite Meltonio's encouragement, Evie and I can't help feeling discouraged as we walk home. I change the subject to the sea life centre. We're both glad we've got something good to look forward to.

Eco-info

As well as being a major part of street litter and world-wide pollution, carrier bags are a long-term problem, even when they go to landfill – plastic can take up to a thousand years to degrade there. So many bags could be reused or recycled or don't need to be used in the first place.

Chapter Four

'Phew!' Evie flumps down on her seat beside me on the coach on Monday. Her eyes, which are bright green like a cat's, are shining, so I know that she is as excited as I am about going on today's school trip to Sandybay Sea Life Centre. Her red hair is mad and messy from rushing, with some bits curling in one direction and some bits curling in another. It reminds me of froth and bubbles, which suits her exuberant personality. I tend to be quieter and more cautious, and my mousey-brown shoulder-length hair hangs like a damp dishcloth when it is not tied back. My eyes are the colour of mud – or chocolate, which is a nicer thought.

'I wish I had hair like yours!' I say, not for the first time.

'But my hair's wild!' Evie exclaims, shaking her

head vigorously from side to side so that her curls whip the side of my face. 'I wish I had nice straight hair like yours!'

'If I had hair like either of you, I would have to hide my head in a brown paper bag,' drawls the familiar, sarcastic voice of Amelia as she pauses beside us. She really is the most conceited and attention-seeking girl in our Year at Shrubberylands Comprehensive. She tends to look down on Evie and me as if we are small crawling things which aren't worthy to get squished under the sole of her expensive designer shoes. But Evie and I aren't bothered by this – we aren't phased by the likes of Amelia! We'd rather be originals than clones of someone so shallow, like the So Cool Girls.

We are more concerned, however, that other people seem to be cold-shouldering us. Evie did well trying to relax and chat normally last week, but I think the protest email didn't go down well. Then, to make matters worse, Evie was so frustrated at the lack of people turning up for the protest that she sent another email to our friends saying how disappointed she was – at least, I hope that they are still our friends! I tried to suggest that it might be a good idea to be a little more understanding, as there may have been very good reasons why they couldn't make it to the protest, apart from them having had enough of our eco-encouragement.

But Evie was not in an understanding mood. She *can* be sympathetic – she is often very good at cheering me up and always willing to listen to my problems – but she seems to have taken our friends' failure to attend the protest to heart.

Amelia has been attempting to make things even worse by telling everyone how pathetic and stupid we looked standing outside Kwikspend on Saturday, and how the manager came and shouted at us – which isn't even true! Fortunately, no one seems inclined to listen to her at the moment – everyone is too excited about going to the sea life centre.

Amelia swishes her long straight hair back over her shoulder, like a blond waterfall, and settles into a seat just behind us with her best friend Jemima, who is one of the group of Amelia wannabes. 'At least we get to wear our own clothes today instead of the horrid slime-green uniform!' I hear Amelia say to Jemima. It is a relief. I am wearing the red skinny jeans which I got for Christmas, and Evie is wearing grey jeans and a blue organic cotton top with little bunched sleeves. We have brought coats as the weather is cold and overcast but, fortunately, dry.

Evie nudges me and giggles. 'Amelia looks as if she's going to a disco, not to a sea life centre!' she whispers. 'She always has to be the centre of attention, but everyone's going to be looking at the sea creatures – not at her!' Glancing back through the gap between the seats, I see what she means. Amelia is a vision in a white and sparkly gold top and skinny white jeans and white high heels. Evie and I are wearing trainers, as Mr Woodsage has warned us that we will be doing a lot of walking. We eagerly discuss what kind of sea creatures we are likely to see. Evie and I tried to look on the sea life centre website last night but there didn't seem to be one.

Miss Peabody, the other geography teacher, is doing a head count, her own head with its untidy bun of brown hair piled on top, bobbing up and down as she makes sure that everyone is on the coach. With her sharp, beaky nose she reminds me of a bird pecking. I tell Evie that I have spotted the Peabody bird, and we get the giggles.

It's over an hour's drive to the centre, which is on the coast. The coach is noisy, with most of the boys occupying the back seats and pulling faces at people in the cars behind. 'They're so immature!' sighs Evie.

Amelia yawns loudly. 'I'm bored out of my mind

already!' she complains. 'A whole day learning about fish – *boring*!'

'I suppose it's better than being stuck in double maths,' Jemima ventures. 'Maybe there'll be dolphins. I like them.'

'They're just big fish,' Amelia replies crossly.

I can feel Evie bristling with annoyance beside me.

'How can you dismiss something as boring when we haven't even got there yet?' she exclaims angrily, twisting round in her seat to glare at Amelia.

'Besides, dolphins aren't fish, they're mammals,' I remark.

'They're *fish*!' Amelia insists. 'They live in water, don't they? So they're fish. Stupid fish.'

'They're definitely not stupid!' I exclaim, angrily. 'They've got the biggest brains of all sea creatures. A dolphin's brain is the same size as a human's,' I add.

'Or ten times bigger than some people's brains!' snaps Evie, staring pointedly at Amelia.

I put my hand on Evie's arm. 'Remember your New Year's resolution to be nice to people!' I whisper to her, giggling.

Evie curls her top lip and settles back into her seat. We block out the rest of the journey – apart from the nuisance factor of Amelia kicking the back

of my seat until I shout at her to stop (she doesn't) –
by sharing my headphones and listening to music on
my iPod.

We are listening to 'Shake Your Green Thing' by
Greenrock when the coach trundles slowly into the
coach park at the sea life centre.

'We're here!' exclaims Evie excitedly, ripping the
ear-piece out of her ear and sitting up very straight. I
am excited, too.

'Whoopee-do,' says Amelia sarcastically. 'Bring on
the fish.'

I notice that the look of excitement on Evie's face
has faded slightly. She looks almost worried.

'What's wrong?' I ask, although I'm also feeling
uneasy.

Evie points at the big sign over the entrance which
should read *Welcome to Sandybay Sea Life Centre* in big
black letters. Instead, it says: *el om t Sa d Bay Sea
Li e ent* as many of the letters are missing, and the
paint is peeling off a big picture of a leaping dolphin
on the sign. 'It looks a bit shabby,' says Evie, disap-
pointedly.

People are still chattering excitedly, but some of
the boys are laughing about the sign and I hear someone say, 'It isn't at all like I was expecting.'

Before they let us off the coach, Miss Peabody gives us a shrill little lecture on good behaviour and Mr Woodsage reminds us that we are representing our school.

'I expect model behaviour,' he says, looking at us all meaningfully through his little round glasses.

'I've done lots of modelling, sir,' Amelia calls out. 'So that won't be a problem.'

Everyone groans, apart from the So Cool Girls, who titter adoringly.

At last the doors open and the coach disgorges its load of chattering students into the car park. Poor Lee, who suffers from motion sickness, makes a mad dash for the nearest boys' loos, and Mr Bunsen the biology teacher, who is also on the trip, goes to make sure that he's all right. The rest of us are herded through the rusty, paint-chipped ticket barriers into the sea life centre, which is quite empty – this must be because its main season hasn't really started yet. And yet there is litter strewn on the ground and the grassy areas are overgrown and unkempt, with a few, mostly broken, picnic benches.

'But how can they let it look like such a dump?' exclaims Evie, sounding both angry and puzzled.

Miss Peabody silences her with a stern look, but

doesn't disagree with her. We are told to stick together in groups and that we must all assemble on the grassy picnic area beside us in one hour's time so that we can have lunch before going to watch a film about larger sea creatures which are too big to be kept in captivity.

'What – you mean, we're not even going to see a dolphin show?' asks Jemima.

'Well, no,' says Miss Peabody. 'It's cruel to keep dolphins in captivity – they're too big. But you can see lots of other interesting creatures – turtles and sea otters, for instance. And there's lots of information on marine life.'

Aisha looks serious. 'Shouldn't all the sea creatures be in the sea?' she asks.

'Well, they are all rescued animals who were in difficulty in the wild. And by studying creatures in captivity we can learn more about them and that is important in generating awareness, preserving their habitats and helping them in the wild,' says Mr Bunsen, who has returned with a pale-looking Lee.

'I suppose so,' says Aisha, who doesn't look completely convinced. 'I hope they're being looked after properly,' she adds, voicing our concerns as we look around at the general shabbiness surrounding us.

'Hopefully all the sea creatures here are as well

cared for as the animals and birds are at the Eco-Gardens,' I suggest, referring to the wildlife park which Evie and I helped to rescue when it was in financial difficulties. 'They just need to . . . er . . . redecorate the place a bit . . .' This is an understatement. The door to a nearby building is hanging off its rusty hinges.

'Come on, Lola!' Evie grabs me by the arm and pulls me along with her into a long, dark building with brightly-lit tanks set into its walls, full of colourful and weird-looking fish. The building smells of damp and Evie says the fish look depressed – although I find it hard to tell. The boys seem particularly fascinated by a tank seething with piranhas, and Lee, who seems fully recovered, wants to know when feeding time is.

I like the tropical fish, and I stand admiring their jewel-like colours while Amelia passes by with her gang of So Cool Girls, her high heels trip-trapping on the stone floor. She's not really looking at anything, but announces 'It smells in here!' in a loud voice. For once, I have to agree with her.

Evie is fascinated by an electric eel. 'It's so weird!' she exclaims. 'But wouldn't it be great if we could somehow harness the energy from an electric eel and use it as an alternative power source? Without harming the eel, of course.'

'Hmm. I think you might need more than one electric eel – you'd probably need millions. So you'd have to build gigantic tanks to keep them in. And you'd have to feed them. It might end up costing even more.'

'OK, OK! Let's forget about electric eel energy!' Evie gives me a playful push.

Emerging from the dark building, Evie and I both blink as our eyes readjust to the light.

'Oh, Evie!' I exclaim. 'Look! They are *sooo* cute!'

We both rush over to a large enclosure containing a pool. On a rock overhanging the pool, three creatures with blunt noses, whiskered faces, thick brown coats and broad tails are lying sprawled, apparently asleep.

'It's the sea otters!' Evie exclaims, reading a notice attached to the wire mesh fence around the enclosure, which is fringed by overgrown bushes with a few pieces of litter stuck in them. 'That one's name is Scooter!'

At the sound of his name, Scooter suddenly sits up, shakes himself, and leaps off his rock onto the earthy bank surrounding his pool.

'Scooter!' squeals Evie. 'Hi, Scooter!'

Scooter stares at us for a moment and then slides

down the bank into his pool for a swim. We spend a long time watching him and the other otters who soon join in, splashing and shooting through the water like torpedoes. Next, Evie takes me by the arm and pulls me over to a large tank containing two turtles. Evie and I are shocked to see that the glass sides of the tank are covered in green algae and that the water looks quite murky. This time I agree with Evie that the turtles look sad.

Soon it is time for everyone to gather at the picnic area for lunch. We have all brought rucksacks with our own packed lunches and drinks. Evie and I have recently been making an effort, as committed eco-worriers, to persuade people to refill water bottles with tap water rather than using them once and then discarding them. A few people seem to have taken this on board, but I notice that many more are stuffing empty plastic bottles in the nearby litterbin. At least they're not dropping them on the ground, so Mrs Baggot would be pleased, but even taking them home to be recycled would be better than stuffing them in the bin, which is overflowing and has obviously not been emptied for a while.

Suddenly there is a piercing shriek from Amelia. 'Eeeeeek! Get it away from me! Get it away!'

An ungainly pelican has waddled towards her from the nearby man-made lake in the middle of the sea life centre, the slack pouch under its long beak wobbling as it walks. It stretches its neck towards Amelia, opening its mouth for food.

In her panic to scramble away from the pelican, Amelia drops her sandwich and the pelican gobbles it up. Everyone roars with laughter.

'It ate my sandwich! Stupid bird!' Amelia squawks indignantly from a safe distance. A sea life centre keeper, dressed in a green polo shirt and beige shorts, shoos the pelican away. Other than the person at the entrance, he is the first member of staff whom we have seen. Apart from the fish and other creatures, the place seems so deserted!

'That pelican's not having *my* sandwich!' says Evie, unwrapping her lunch.

'What have you got?' I ask.

'I've got a roasted vegetable wrap with humous – Dad made it.'

'Wow! I wish my dad made things like that! He can barely boil an egg. But Evie . . .'

'Yes?'

'Are you a vegetarian, or aren't you?'

'I told you, I'm a part-time vegetarian. I have

days off.' Evie munches happily, as I take a bite of my wholemeal cheese scone. I may keep my apple for the journey home. 'But today,' she continues, 'I'm in a vegetarian mood.'

'It's strange,' I remark, 'you were the one who persuaded me to become a vegetarian when I wasn't really sure about it. And now I'm more of a vegetarian than you are. I haven't eaten meat since last year when we saved Samson from being served up as Christmas dinner.'

'I know, and I really admire you, Lola. But Dad's Sunday roasts are so good – I really can't bear the thought of giving them up forever!'

Mr Woodsage tells everyone to hurry up as it is nearly time for the film on Cetaceans. He explains that this is a group of animals which include whales, porpoises and dolphins. People start packing their lunch containers away quickly as everyone – apart from Amelia – is keen to see the dolphin film.

On our way to the cinema we pass through an underground tunnel with a huge dirty glass window where visitors can watch some fish and turtles swimming around. On the walls of the tunnel there is a faded exhibition explaining about the dolphins in their natural habitat. Some of the posters in the grimy display cases have mould growing on them, but we are still able to read about the threats to marine wildlife.

Evie and I are dismayed to read that one of the greatest threats to dolphins and other sea creatures such as turtles is being caught in fishing nets. Another threat to dolphins is from commercial fishing which causes long-term problems for dolphin populations because their food supply is over-fished.

'Oh no!' I exclaim. 'Look at this, Evie! This is even worse!' Evie and I read about the threat to marine wildlife from pollution.

'Mr Woodsage told us about the rubbish vortex in the Pacific Ocean. Do you remember? It's twice the size of Texas – a huge mass of rubbish made up of plastic junk, including footballs, kayaks, Lego blocks and carrier bags, and it's kept together by swirling underwater currents.'

'Oh – look at this!' I say in a small voice. I seem to have a ping-pong ball in my throat. I swallow hard and force it down. There is a photo of a poor dolphin with a plastic bag wrapped around its snout. Beside the photo is an explanation that the dolphin died of starvation after its beak became entangled in the bag and it could no longer feed. It goes on to say that turtles mistake plastic bags for jellyfish, which they then eat, and die when their stomachs become full of plastic.

'You and I are eco-worriers – we should be doing *something* to stop it!'

'It's not as if we haven't tried – what about our campaign outside Kwikspend?' Evie reminds me. 'But obviously we need to do more – much more!' she adds, fervently. 'And I wish we could do something to help this place, too!'

Suddenly I realise that we are the only two people still looking at the exhibition as everyone else has rushed through the tunnel in order to get to the cinema.

The cinema is just as shabby as the rest of the sea life centre, and some of the seats are broken. Everyone laughs when Lee's seat collapses and he finds himself sitting on the floor. Miss Peabody tells us to 'Shush!' as the film is about to begin.

The film itself is scratched in places and jumps around a bit, and the sound quality is strange, sounding muffled throughout. But there are enough beautiful shots of leaping dolphins for everyone to go 'Ooh!' and 'Aah!' at regular intervals. Everyone is entranced as we see them swimming in groups and gliding through the sea as if they are flying underwater.

'I'd love to see dolphins in the ocean,' I say to Evie.

'Me, too,' she agrees. 'Oh, look!' she gasps.

The dolphins in the film are speeding like silent torpedoes underwater again, and then their fins thrust towards the surface, launching them out of the water in a burst of white spray. Their bodies arch clear and one of them flips to the right, one to the left, and one straight ahead. There is a great splash and a fountain of bright water sprays on to the camera lens. There is an outburst of squealing, laughter and applause.

'Oh, for goodness' sake!' Amelia exclaims in outraged tones. 'They're only overgrown fish!'

Everyone ignores her and cheers as the dolphins leap and flip backwards together, diving, twisting and jumping once more.

When the film has finished, Jed, the keeper, asks if anyone has any questions. Shaheen wants to know more about the reasons for not keeping dolphins at the sea life centre.

'Because no self-respecting dolphin would want to live in a dump like this!' Lee mutters under his breath, before a look from Miss Peabody silences him.

Jed, who did not seem to hear Lee's comment, explains that the sea creatures in the film, which featured whales and sharks as well as dolphins, are too large to be housed in the sea life centre.

'I agree!' says Evie, nodding. 'It would be cruel to keep such huge creatures in captivity!'

'It's an eco-no-no!' I comment.

Jed adds that too much contact between humans and dolphins spreads diseases, although people can sometimes swim with wild dolphins in specially supervised conditions.

Evie asks about pollution in the sea and how it affects the creatures we've just seen, and Jed tells us in detail about rubbish, and especially plastic, being a huge problem. He says that the sea life centre used to run conservation projects such as a clear-up-on-the-beach campaign, but at the moment it is too short of money to fund the projects. There are fewer visitors than there used to be.

'I would have thought it was obvious why there aren't many visitors,' Evie whispers to me. 'People are put off by the sea life centre's shabby appearance. They don't want to come here. And others probably don't know about it – the publicity's non-existent. There isn't even a website! Why don't they do something about it?'

When the question-and-answer session comes to an end, she drags me along with her to talk to Jed. Aisha comes, too. Suddenly, Evie blurts out in a loud voice, 'Why is the sea life centre so run down? Wouldn't it encourage more people to come if it looked better?'

Jed looks taken aback and Evie looks slightly embarrassed but defiant. Aisha is nodding agreement with Evie and other people are exchanging what sound like murmurs of agreement.

Jed frowns slightly, then hesitates, considering his answer carefully. He explains that the owners of the sea life centre are an elderly couple called Mr and Mrs Burlington. They are not in the best of health and they have had to devote most of their time and money to their son, who was left paralysed and in a wheelchair since a car accident nearly two years ago.

'They just don't have the time or the energy – or the money – to run this place properly,' Jed explains, sadly. 'There are a few members of staff – including myself – who have been prepared to stay on and work for a minimum wage. But I really don't know what's going to happen . . .' Jed's voice trails off. I am sure that I see tears in the corner of his eyes.

Mr Woodsage tells us that it is time to thank Jed and say goodbye, as we have to get on the coach and return to school.

Reluctantly, we leave, paying a brief visit to the

rather dusty gift shop, where I buy a little blue dolphin pendant necklace, which I immediately put on, and Evie buys a small dolphin wind-chime.

'I wish I had loads of money!' I say. 'I'd give it all to the sea life centre – it could be so great.'

'Me, too,' agrees Evie, fervently.

On the coach coming home, Lee cracks fish joke after fish joke, suggesting that we all stage an 'o-fish-al' protest about the terrible state the sea life centre is in. 'It's an awful plaice!' he exclaims. 'A plaice is a fish – geddit?' he says, nudging me with his elbow. I am sitting between him and Evie at the back of the coach. Everyone is laughing, apart from Evie, Aisha and me. I feel really sorry that the sea life centre is so run-down.

'But seriously, we should do something,' says Evie. Our friends nod agreement and start trying to think of ways that they can help.

Suddenly I realise something. I nudge Evie. 'Everyone loves dolphins. They've all been bored about our efforts to be green but, if we link eco-problems to dolphin problems, we'll get them interested again.'

Evie nods and smiles in hope. We no longer feel that we are on our own in our wish to make the world a better place! It is as though the awe and admiration that everyone feels for the dolphins has broken down barriers between us and our friends – we all now have a shared interest and common goal.

Well, nearly all of us. Only Amelia complains all the way home about being cold and fed up with fish.

Eco-info

No matter how lovely it is to see dolphins up close, no captive facility is able to provide the space and behavioural needs of a dolphin. In the wild, dolphins can live in groups (called pods) of up to a thousand dolphins, and swim 50 miles a day – no comparison to a tank and a few other dolphins.

A dolphin's smile is just the way its face is made and doesn't relate to how a dolphin is feeling.

Chapter Five

'If I hear the word "dolphin" once more, I shall go mad!' exclaims Liam, covering his ears with his hands.

'DOLPHIN!' Evie and I both shout at him together.

Liam goes cross-eyed and pretends to strangle himself. We are in the kitchen at Evie's house and have been talking about dolphins and the sea life centre ever since we got back from the trip.

Evie's mum laughs. 'I like hearing about the dolphins,' she says. 'I do feel sorry for the owners and their son – it does sound very run-down. I really hope something can be done to help them.'

'Oh, so do we,' I reply.

'Come on!' says Evie to me. 'Let's go and see if there's a reply to that email I sent Kate.'

As soon as we got home earlier, Evie rushed straight up to her room and sent an email to Kate Meadowsweet, who is our friend and the owner of the Eco-Gardens. Kate knows a great deal about creatures of all kinds, and we are hoping that she will have some ideas about what can be done to help the sea life centre, especially since she was in a similar situation a while ago when the Eco-Gardens was short of money and visitors and faced closure.

'It is a bit different though, isn't it?' I say to Evie. 'I mean, the Eco-Gardens has always been really well run, but this place, well, it's not great, is it? Part of me thinks it ought to be shut down.'

While Evie sits at the computer, I hear her dolphin wind-chime near her window. It tinkles gently and catches the light as the little dolphins slowly twirl around.

'Yes!' exclaims Evie. 'There's a reply from Kate.' I crane my neck over Evie's shoulder to read the email.

Kate tells us that she is very sorry to hear about the problems that the sea life centre is facing and that she would like to help. She visited it a few years ago and it seemed quite well run then, and had been very involved in protecting coastlines and highlighting conservation problems, but obviously it's fallen on hard times. She says that she has a friend, Todd McHenry, who runs a fantastic aquarium in Florida which specialises in rehabilitating ill and trapped sea creatures. It's very different from the sea life centre, of course, but he is an astute businessman who has good ideas about turning around ailing businesses and making them thrive. She gives us his email address and the website address of his centre – it's called the Dolphin Dreams Center (she reminds us that, as it's in America, centre is spelled with an 'er' at the end), as he is a particular expert on dolphins.

'What a lovely name!' I exclaim. We immediately send an email to Todd McHenry at the Dolphin Dreams Center, telling him that we are friends of Kate Meadowsweet, and we really hope that he can give us some advice about what to do about the crumbling sea life centre.

'Let's look at the Dolphin Dreams Center website,' I say, eagerly.

It looks beautiful, with blue skies, palm trees, and dolphins leaping out of the ocean. There are also pictures of porpoises and whales. There is even a photo of Todd McHenry himself, a square-jawed man with a thick thatch of dark hair and piercing blue eyes, and a dazzling white smile, which contrasts with his bronzed skin. There are details of the education programmes his aquarium runs, as well as hospitals to rehabilitate ill or stranded sea creatures before returning them to the wild. There are also details of dolphin watches and swimming with wild dolphins in a carefully regulated, eco-friendly way, which he organises.

'I'd love to swim with dolphins,' I say.

'Oh, so would I,' Evie agrees fervently. 'I hope Todd gets back to us soon. Wouldn't it be great if he really wanted to help the sea life centre? And it would be so great if he threw in an all-expenses-paid trip to Florida for you and me to see the dolphins in the wild – and swim with them!'

'Er, Evie, I think you might be getting a bit carried away! We're only asking for advice!'

'Todd looks like he could solve any problem!' exclaims Evie. 'He's very good-looking. Not that he's my type, of course. Too old.'

'He is quite fit,' I agree, giggling. Todd McHenry looks like a Hollywood film star – the sort who appears in celebrity magazines and is regularly besieged by screaming female fans. 'But you're right – he is a bit old. I just hope he can tell us what to do about the sea life centre. He must be very busy though.'

'The owners just seem too tired to think of ideas,' says Evie. 'Jed told us that they're elderly and not very well. They probably haven't got enough money to advertise the sea life centre properly. I certainly hadn't heard about it before we went there.'

I touch the little blue dolphin charm around my neck. It's now my favourite piece of jewellery ever.

'So let's plan some fundraising activities,' I say. 'We can raise money for the sea life centre and sea life in general.'

Evie looks thoughtful. 'We could organise a sponsored litter-pick around the town,' she suggests.

'Er – Evie? I don't know if you noticed, but people weren't wildly enthusiastic about picking up litter last time you suggested it,' I point out.

'I know. But everyone loves dolphins. I was talking to people on the coach coming home and a lot of them had seen that awful picture of the poor dolphin which starved to death because of the plastic bag tangled round its beak. People were really upset by it – Aisha was in tears. So I'm thinking that everyone will be a lot more willing to pick up litter now, knowing that dolphins and turtles starve to death and choke on plastic bags and other rubbish.

We've got to carry on with our plastics campaign – but we'll do it as part of Do It for the Dolphins. And let's try to save the sea life centre – not just for the owners, but because it will enthuse people about dolphins, too!'

'I see what you mean,' I say, warming up to this new approach. 'Do It for the Dolphins – that's a good phrase. So, if we relate our eco-message to dolphins, people will be more receptive than if we drone on about it and try to make people feel guilty, as we have been doing.'

'Exactly! Although I'm sure I don't drone. Do I?'

'Sometimes. Just a little. No! No – you don't drone at all! Honestly!' Evie is attacking me with a pillow. Soon we are having a full-scale eco-worriers' pillow-fight, before collapsing, laughing, on the bed.

'I think we should have a fun activity as well,' I say, when I have recovered my breath. 'Something which people will really enjoy doing, and which will raise money for the sea life centre.'

Evie agrees. 'Sponsored pillow-fights?'

I giggle. 'That would be fun! It's worth thinking about. But we need something that people can easily do at school – whacking each other with pillows might not be quite right. I think we need to think of something which is directly related to dolphins. I know! How about a competition to write the best poem about dolphins? People could pay fifty pence to enter.'

'You like writing poetry, but not many people do. It sounds a bit like homework. We've already got to write a report on our visit to the sea life centre,' she replies.

'But this would be fun!'

'If you say so.' Evie sounds unconvinced.

'Lots of people enjoy writing poetry,' I persist. 'It's worth a try, at least.'

'OK – you can suggest it at school tomorrow. And we'll ask Mr Woodsage to help us to get the sponsored litter-pick properly organised. Won't it be amazing if we can get everyone clearing up the whole town?'

'It really will!' I say.

I decide to go home as I want to tell Mum and Dad all about the dolphins and our trip to the sea life centre.

As Evie and I leave her room, Liam is coming upstairs and stops to stare at us. 'You're not still going on about dolphins, are you?' he asks.

'Yes!' we reply.

Liam groans. 'I may have to go and live at the

North Pole,' he says. 'There are no dolphins at the North Pole – and no sisters, or their friends.'

'Dolphins are swimming further north,' says Evie. 'Because of climate change. They'll probably reach the North Pole, if all the ice melts.'

'Aargh! There's no escape!' cries Liam.

I feel puzzled. 'Don't you like dolphins, Liam?' I ask.

'Dolphins are OK,' Liam replies. 'But I know from experience that when my sister gets one of her obsessions, the whole family somehow gets involved and no one talks about anything else. And now it's dolphins!'

'I'm not obsessed!' exclaims Evie, indignantly. 'I'm passionate! You'd be passionate about dolphins, too, if you knew anything about them. Remember how fond you became of Samson the pig after you met him?'

Liam shrugs. 'Whatever,' he says. 'I'm probably more of a pig man than a dolphin man.' And he disappears into his room, closing the door behind him.

'Hopeless,' sighs Evie, shaking her head.

I arrive at my house at the same time as Dad, who is arriving back in the car with some milk and bread. 'Hello!' he says, smiling at me. His eyes are brown like mine, but his hair is a lighter shade of brown, receding and grey round the edges.

'Dad!' I exclaim. 'Did you use the car just to go round the corner to the corner shop? That is *sooo* un-eco-friendly! Why don't you walk or cycle?'

Dad sighs, and rolls his eyes at me. He looks tired.

'Oh – sorry, Dad. I don't mean to nag,' I apologise.

I really must remember that gentle persuasion is better than full-on nagging – this is the message I am trying to get through to Evie, so I really ought to practise what I preach.

'But Dad?'

'Yes, Lola?'

'Will you at least reuse or recycle that plastic carrier bag so that it doesn't end up choking a dolphin or turtle?'

Dad looks surprised, but he agrees to my request. Then we go indoors and I tell Mum and Dad all about my day.

Later in the evening, Evie emails me to say that she has had an amazing idea. She thinks that we should plan a Dolphin Day at school to raise funds for the sea life centre and sea creatures. She suggests that everything on Dolphin Day should have a dolphin theme.

'I'm thinking cakes decorated with dolphins,

dolphin pictures, dolphin books, dolphin jewellery and dolphin poetry recitals, a play about dolphins, guess-the-name-of-the-cuddly-dolphin, a dolphin lucky dip, a dolphin exhibition, raffle, tombola, and information about the sea life centre,' she writes.

She seems to be buzzing with ideas. I feel quite tired after reading her email, although I like the idea of Dolphin Day. I email back to say that I think that a Dolphin Day would be really popular and that we should definitely Do It for the Dolphins.

I can hear the tumble-dryer rumbling away. I wonder whether I should remind Mum that a tumble dryer is an environmental disaster, accounting for half a tonne or more of CO_2 a year. Should I tell her that I have noticed that she has used it three times in the last week, instead of hanging the washing on the line? But I don't want to nag. And I have also noticed that Mum has been very good recently about reusing plastic bags. So perhaps she deserves to be spared an eco-worrier lecture tonight.

I decide to have a shower instead.

The following day at school we talk to Mr Woodsage about our plans to raise money for the sea life centre. Mr Woodsage is very encouraging as he is just as concerned as we are about the dilapidated state of the sea life centre, and agrees that it would be good to do something to help.

He likes the idea of the sponsored litter-pick, and says that he will talk to the town council and get it properly organised. Then he will get sponsorship forms printed and we can help to get as many people as possible involved. And he's very keen on Dolphin Day. He suggests a Saturday in a few weeks' time. He is equally enthusiastic about my idea to hold a dolphin poem competition, and suggests that we should ask Miss Spelling, the popular new English teacher, to judge it.

As we anticipated, people are much more willing to get involved in the fund-raising activities now that it's connected with dolphins. Even people from other Years who didn't go on the trip to the sea life centre are attracted by the idea of saving the lives of dolphins and turtles and other sea creatures. They are shocked when we tell them about dolphins and turtles dying because of plastic waste, and many people are keen to take part in the sponsored litter-pick. The phrase 'Do It for the Dolphins!' rapidly catches on, and soon everyone is saying, 'Do It for the Dolphins!'

I have mixed reactions to my idea for a dolphin

poem competition. A few people scream and run out of the room at the very thought of writing poetry, and others pull bored faces and turn their backs on me as if writing poetry is uncool to the point of embarrassing.

'So what's the prize?' Lee wants to know.

'Prize?' I query, realising that I hadn't thought about this.

'Yes,' says Lee. 'If I'm going to pay fifty pence to pen a brilliant poem, I want to know what prize I'm going to win.'

I look at Evie desperately. Everyone seems to be looking at me expectantly, waiting to hear what the prize is going to be. If I say that it is something pathetic like a chocolate bar, I'm worried that people may lose interest – not that they've shown any so far anyway.

Evie is staring back at me and chewing her lip. This is a sure sign that she is thinking hard. I know she wants to help me. Suddenly she starts gabbling: 'Ah – yes! The prize! The *prize*! It's a very special prize. Very special indeed!'

'Yes?' says Lee, questioningly. 'What is it?'

I think I see a thought bubble above Evie's head with a light bulb – an eco-friendly energy-saving light bulb – in it, which lights up – PING! – as inspiration strikes her.

'The prize,' she says, 'the very special prize is that the winning poem will be set to music by my brother Liam, who will perform it at his next gig with the Rock Hyraxes. And . . . and – who knows? – it may even be released as a single to raise even more money to help dolphins!' Evie stops, looking slightly flushed. There is a collective gasp of amazement.

My mouth is hanging open and everyone around me is exclaiming excitedly. Liam is very popular, and his band – the Rock Hyraxes – are considered very cool. Everyone loves them and now everyone is saying they want their poem to be set to music by Liam!

Taking Evie by the arm, I pull her to one side for a quiet word . . .

'Um . . . Evie? Have you by any chance talked to Liam about any of this?' I ask, although I think I already know the answer.

'Er . . . not yet,' Evie replies, quietly. 'But you've got to admit, it's a good idea.'

'It's a very good idea. I'm just not sure whether Liam will think it's such a good idea. Remember what he was saying about always getting dragged into your obsessions?'

'Don't have a go at me!' Evie retorts angrily. 'I just got you out of a difficult situation when you couldn't think of a prize, and now everyone wants to enter the dolphin poem competition. You should be grateful to me!'

'Oh, Evie, I am! I really am! I just hope you can sort this out with Liam.'

'No problem!' says Evie, airily, although the expression on her face definitely says *PROBLEM*!

Eco-info

We use an estimated 10 billion plastic bags a year in the UK. On average, that's about 167 per person. Make the decision to use fewer - if lots of people make a small change, big things can happen! It's worth remembering too that plastic bags were only invented in the 1950s and were rarely used until the late 1970s. . . .

Chapter Six

We spend the next couple of weeks preparing for Dolphin Day. There is huge enthusiasm for the idea of Dolphin Day and everyone is getting involved, apart from Amelia and the So Cool Girls, who stand on the sidelines making rude remarks about stinking fish. I don't think Amelia will ever understand that a dolphin is a mammal. They are definitely not fish as they need to come to the surface to breathe.

We are in Evie's room, staying out of her brother's way, and sifting through the poetry competition entries, which have been flooding in.

When Evie told Liam she had volunteered him to set a dolphin poem to music as a prize in a competition, he was furious. 'You did *what?*' he said. I think he said a lot of other things as well, but Evie didn't hang around to hear them. She came round to my house, where she stayed for the rest of the evening.

'At least we've already raised some money to help the sea life centre,' I say, feeling pleased at our success. 'It's not enough, of course, but it's a start. Some of them are quite funny, and others are really sad. A lot of them seem to be about dolphins choking on plastic bags and dying. Do you think Liam *will* set the winning poem to music?'

Evie shrugs. 'If he doesn't, I'm dead,' she says, matter-of-factly. 'People won't forgive me for offering a prize like that and then withdrawing it.'

'Did you mention that to Liam?'

'Yes. He said I deserved to die. But I think he'll calm down. I think he'll probably do it.'

'We'd better be really nice to him.'

Evie nods. 'I'm already being nice to him,' she says. 'This morning he left a tap running and I *didn't* tell him off for wasting water.'

'That was nice of you.'

'I thought so.' Evie picks up one of the poems, written on a scruffy piece of paper torn out of an exercise book, and reads it with a look of disgust on her face.

'Well – that's nice!' she exclaims sarcastically, handing

it to me. The poem is by Amelia, who has signed her name at the bottom in pink ink with a lot of curly flourishes. The poem reads:

A dolphin is a stupid fish
But I wouldn't eat it
If it was served on a dish.
So shut up about dolphins!
That's my greatest wish.

'That's a really awful poem,' I comment. 'I don't think she'll be winning any prizes for that one. With any luck, it'll get her into trouble with Miss Spelling!'

Evie is reading another of the poems. 'I like this one,' she says. 'It's by Aisha.'

Evie hands me the poem, and I read it aloud:

'White spray
Flash of grey
Leaping dolphins
Make my day.
No more plastic
In their way
Let the dolphins
Dance and play.
Let the dolphins play
Oh let the dolphins play!'

'I like it,' I agree. 'It's quite short, though. Some of

these poems are really long.'

'I expect Liam would prefer a shorter one to set to music,' comments Evie, checking her email, which has bleeped to say that she has a message.

'It's from Todd McHenry! He's coming over to the UK. He wants to visit the sea life centre on Saturday and wonders if we can come with him! He said that hearing us mention Kate reminded him that it had been too long since he last saw her, and he would like to come on a visit. He hopes to be able to give some helpful advice to the "folks at the sea life centre".'

Evie and I hug each other, laughing excitedly.

'He must really want to help, if he's prepared to come all that way!' I exclaim.

'Yes – but he's mainly coming to see Kate, I think,' says Evie. 'But it's great that he's coming at all. I want to ask him loads of questions about the aquarium in Florida – he must know such a lot about dolphins! Oh, it's really exciting! We're going to meet a Hollywood star!'

'Er, Evie? He's a conservationist and he's from Florida.'

'Yes, but he *looks* like a Hollywood star! He says he is looking forward to meeting us as we sound like very caring young people, and he understands our concern about the sea life centre.'

'He does sound really nice,' I say.

'Yes,' Evie agrees. 'He should be able to give loads of advice. Let's email Kate – she must know he's coming already. And let's look at the Dolphin Dreams Center website again – it's so cool!'

We have visited Todd McHenry's aquarium website several times already as it's so fascinating. The fish are kept in beautifully clean, dramatically lit tanks in state-of-the-art buildings, some with glass floors and ceilings so that you can see the fish swimming above and below you as if you are in the ocean with them. There is soft music playing to add to the dreamlike atmosphere, which the website tells us that the centre provides to make the visitor's experience more pleasurable. Visitors can also wear a headset and listen to a commentary telling them all about the fish.

'Looking at this just make me even more aware of how awful the sea life centre is,' Evie comments, shaking her head sadly.

'Let's look at the bit about watching the wild dolphins,' I suggest as we browse the website. This part of the website has a heading: *The ocean is not our home . . . we are guests and should act accordingly.*

There is a short video of Todd McHenry himself

explaining that the Dolphin Dreams Center offers trips to small groups of people in a glass-bottomed boat to watch the dolphins. Sometimes people are allowed to get in the water with the dolphins, as long as they show proper respect for them. The most important thing, Todd says, is to splash as little as possible and, if a wild dolphin approaches you, you should not reach out to touch. Dolphins have a very acute sense of touch, and touching or grabbing a dolphin is guaranteed to push them away. You can swim alongside the dolphins, but you must always respect their personal space and never swim in a way that could be potentially distressing for them.

'Oh, I would *never* distress a dolphin!' Evie exclaims. 'If only I could swim with them, I'd be *soooooooo* respectful!'

'Oh, me too!' I agree.

The rest of the week drags by, as Evie and I are yearning to get to Saturday so that we can see Kate, meet Todd McHenry, and visit the sea life centre again. It is a relief to hand all the poetry competition entries over to Miss Spelling as we are beginning to feel overwhelmed by poetry. But we have raised forty-seven pounds and fifty pence – some people entered the competition twice or even three times, paying fifty pence each time – and we are looking forward to handing this amount over to the owners of the sea life centre.

Liam has been hiding in the Sixth Form Common Room, as every time he emerges people have been coming up to him and reciting poems about dolphins to him, insisting that their poems are the best to set to music.

Evie has been steering clear of Liam at home and hiding away on her computer. When she checks her email on Friday, she finds one from Kate. She tells us that Todd would like to take us all out to lunch tomorrow, before we go to the sea life centre. Kate has suggested that we go to Samson's Bistro.

'Cool!' Evie and I exclaim.

Saturday is bright and sunny. I wake up early and go for a run, enjoying the early-morning birdsong. It feels warm and almost springlike.

At last it is eleven-thirty! Kate comes to Evie's house to collect us in one of the Eco-Gardens' eco-friendly animal-dung-powered vans. Kate and Todd McHenry step out of the van so that Kate can introduce Todd to Evie's parents and to us. Our parents know Kate really well, so are happy to let us all go out for lunch.

Todd is very tall, and even more bronzed than he appeared in his photo, due to being outside in the Florida sunshine all the time. His teeth seem even whiter, probably due to expensive dental work. His blue eyes shine with friendliness and he has a firm handshake. He is not wearing a wedding ring.

I decide that he and Kate, who is very pretty, with a shower of blond curls, should get married. But I'm not sure if this thought has occurred to either of them.

Todd wanted to invite our parents to join us for lunch, but Evie's parents have already been invited somewhere else and my parents are busy with their work putting up a marquee at a classic car rally taking place this weekend.

Meltonio welcomes us warmly to Samson's Bistro.

'Has Delilah had her piglets yet?' Evie asks him, eagerly.

'Not yet. But they are due any day now!' Meltonio replies, beaming, his black moustache rippling. He shows us to our table.

Over lunch, Todd asks us lots of questions about the sea life centre. Evie is uncharacteristically quiet to start with – perhaps she is overawed by his

Hollywood-star looks! But Todd is very friendly and we soon start talking. We tell him how fantastic the dolphin film was, but also how run-down the place is. We also talk to him and Kate about our fund-raising ideas and how there is going to be a Dolphin Day at school in two weeks' time. They both think that it is an excellent idea and Kate suggests that we ask local businesses to donate gifts for the raffle. She offers tickets for a family day out at the Eco-Gardens and says that there are some items from the Eco-Gardens' gift shop which she can also donate. We thank her profusely.

We tell Todd that we have been looking at the Dolphin Dreams Center website and that we are both fascinated by the thought of watching dolphins and swimming with them. He asks if we are good swimmers and we tell him that we are – I train in the local pool every week, as I want to be an Olympic swimmer. Todd says that it's necessary to be a strong swimmer and that the best way to swim is to adopt as fluid and graceful a style as you can, by wearing flip-pers and keeping your arms by your sides, behind your back, or across your chest, adopting the dolphins' style of swimming.

'That sounds really cool!' I exclaim.

Todd smiles. 'But sometimes it's better just to watch them from the boat,' says Todd. 'We never force in-water encounters on the dolphins. Respect is the key to any interaction. Dolphins must initiate any interaction and have the right to terminate it. Sometimes they do not even come that close and people have to learn to respect that too. Most of the time, people simply snorkel in the water and watch the dolphins swim past around or underneath them.'

It is fascinating listening to Todd talking about the creatures he so clearly loves. Evie and I are both so excited we can hardly eat our Samson's Special Chocolate Ice-cream Indulgence which we have chosen for dessert. But somehow we manage.

Before we leave, we ask Meltonio if he will bring his ice-cream van to Dolphin Day, and he says he will. His brother Luigi, who is the head chef at Samson's, offers to donate a ticket for a romantic meal for two at Samson's. I would like Kate and Todd to win that one!

Then we set off for the sea life centre. We enjoy sitting in the back of the van, listening to Kate and Todd chat about old times and exchange stories about the creatures in their care.

When we reach the sea life centre, which looks even more run-down under the cold leaden-grey sky, I see that an elderly, white-haired couple are waiting just outside the entrance, with a man in a wheelchair. These must be the owners of the sea life centre and their son.

They greet us warmly, but their faces are lined and careworn. Their son has light brown hair and a friendly smile, but as soon as he stops smiling I think he looks sad. The owners' names are Bill and Betty Burlington, and their son's name is Robert – Bob, for short.

They usher us into the sea life centre and start showing us all around. It is clear that they love the centre, but they don't really have the money or energy to put into it to make it really good.

I look around for Jed but he is nowhere to be seen.

'All our money goes on food and running costs,' says Betty Burlington, with a sigh. 'I wish we could afford repairs and redecoration – but we can't . . .' Her voice trails away and she looks frail and old. 'And we have to be close to the hospital for Bob to have his physiotherapy – and Bill has to have treatment for his problems . . .'

'Oh, come along, dear!' exclaims Bill, trying hard to sound cheerful. 'Our guests don't want to hear about our woes – especially not my silly problems! It's a terrible business getting old!' he adds, with a rather hollow chuckle.

We all nod sympathetically.

Evie and I tell them about all our plans to raise money with Dolphin Day. I suddenly feel silly producing our cheque for forty-seven pounds and fifty pence from the poetry competition, made out to the sea life centre – Dad exchanged all the coins we collected for a cheque, as I would have felt even sillier handing over a handful of coins. They obviously need an awful lot more money than that to sort out their problems. But Bill and Betty thank us. I am also a bit worried what we will do if Liam continues to refuse to provide the prize, but I don't say anything. I explain that the money comes from people at our school.

'We all enjoyed our visit to the sea life centre a few weeks ago,' I say. 'And we really want to help. We raised this money by holding a poetry competition, and we're going to have a sponsored litter-pick soon around our town as well as having a Dolphin Day . . .'

Bill and Betty seem very pleased about all our ideas, but I can't help thinking that they need much more help than we can give them.

On the way back, Todd expresses his concern about the sea life centre. He says that it can't carry on like that.

'Can't you think of how to help?' I ask desperately.

But Todd just runs through the list of what needs doing. It is not a small list.

Suddenly all our money-raising activities seem rather feeble – and a waste of time if it's going to close anyway. Evie and I are both very quiet on the journey. I don't know what we'd been expecting really – maybe that Todd would come up with loads of wonderful ideas – but he and Kate just talk about how very run-down the sea life centre seems.

'Oh dear – has someone died?' Liam asks, noticing our downcast expressions as we walk into Evie's kitchen after Kate has dropped us off.

Evie bursts into tears and her mum rushes over to put her arms round her. 'Whatever's wrong?' she asks.

Between sobs, Evie says how feeble all our efforts are to raise money for the sea life centre. Even though everyone's enthusiastic about Dolphin Day, she realises it's never going to make enough money. This is very unlike Evie – she's usually really enthusiastic about everything.

Liam looks genuinely sorry. 'Tell you what,' he says, attempting to cheer his sister up. 'I've decided I don't mind setting a dolphin poem to music. So I'll do it – OK?'

Evie nods and smiles wanly. She fetches us two drinks of banana and strawberry smoothie from the fridge and we take them upstairs to her room. In spite of what Liam said, we don't seem able to cheer ourselves up.

Liam comes running up the stairs and pokes his head round the bedroom door. Evie hands him the piece of paper with the winning poem on it. He reads the poem slowly, frowning.

'*White spray*
Flash of grey
Leaping dolphins
Make my day.
No more plastic
In their way
Let the dolphins
Dance and play.
Let the dolphins play
Oh let the dolphins play!'

As we had hoped, Miss Spelling had chosen Aisha's poem as the winner of the poetry competition. Aisha is very excited at the thought of having her poem set to music by Liam. She has decided that the poem should be called 'Dolphin Dream', as it sounds like a good name for a song, too.

Liam reads it again, still frowning. Then he mutters something inaudible and disappears into his room, staring hard at the piece of paper.

He stays there for nearly an hour. We hear him strum a few chords on his guitar and we also hear him say a few rude words.

'I think he's in the throes of musical creativity,' Evie remarks.

When Liam eventually emerges from his room, she asks him brightly if he has set the poem to music yet.

'No,' he replies, shortly, and leaves to go to his job, working evening shifts as a waiter at Samson's.

It's the end of the school week and Liam has apparently been in the throes of musical creativity for much of it.

Evie tells me that he has stayed in his room a lot more than usual, strumming chords and occasionally exclaiming loudly in frustration. He has broken at least two guitar strings and come down for meals in a foul mood. At times she has been scared to speak to him.

'It doesn't sound as though it's going very well,' I remark.

Evie shrugs. 'I don't know,' she says. 'Aisha keeps asking me if her poem's been set to music yet and I have to say, "Liam's still working on it. I'm sure he just wants to make sure his music does your poem justice".'

She tries to sound upbeat and enthusiastic, but I can tell she's still a bit down, unlike her usual exuberant self, even though plans and preparations for Dolphin Day are progressing. I do share her anxiety, though, that everything we are doing won't be enough to save the sea life centre. It makes me wonder if it's even worth bothering with at all.

We hear Liam emerge from his room and Evie rushes out to try and find out how setting the poem to music is going. Judging by the way Liam refuses to answer, and leaves the house without another word, it isn't progressing at all. What are we going to tell Aisha? This is not encouraging – and Evie and I could do with some encouragement!

It's Saturday afternoon, and Evie and I are in her kitchen drinking smoothies and listening to the Dave Groover afternoon show on Shrubberylands FM. I stayed with Evie last night for an eco-worriers' sleepover, but we were both too worried about the sea life centre to enjoy the traditional eco-worriers' pillowfight. We got up late today and have not done very much. Tomorrow it's the sponsored litter-pick and lots of people are taking part. I'm glad about this because it shows that people are genuinely concerned about the plight of the dolphins and other sea creatures. At least Evie and I are getting our eco-worriers' message across, even if the sea life centre is doomed.

The familiar cheery voice of Dave Groover is babbling away in the background. But suddenly something he says makes us both sit bolt upright and listen hard.

'Do you like dolphins as much as I do?' says Dave Groover. 'Are you aware that wild dolphins are still perishing on a daily basis because of all the plastic rubbish that we humans carelessly throw away? It's true! Even our litter here in the UK affects them in the Pacific Ocean. It's one world, groovers. But I'm really glad to tell you that the young people at Shrubberylands Comprehensive want to do something about it! They'll be having a sponsored litter-pick around the town this Sunday – so go on! Sponsor them! And next weekend they're having a Dolphin Day at their school – so go along and support them and help save the dolphins! And that's not all, folks! Someone's just dropped in a CD to the Shrubberylands FM studio, and it's a poem about dolphins by Aisha Lindsay who goes to Shrubberylands

Comprehensive, and it's been set to music by Liam Evans, who's performing it with his band, the Rock Hyraxes. It's called "Dolphin Dream" and I think you're going to love it – so sit back and listen.'

Evie and I stare at each other, open-mouthed with astonishment. We had no idea that Liam had written the music, let alone recorded it!

We listen to Liam singing Aisha's poem and playing his guitar along with his band. It sounds really good! It has quite a hard rock edge so that Liam manages to avoid sounding soppy, singing about dolphins – but you can just about hear Aisha's lyrics.

As soon as the song has finished, Evie calls Liam to tell him that she's just heard it, and it's *awesome*. 'But . . . How . . .?' Her voice trails off incoherently.

I hear Liam laugh over the phone. After a short conversation, Evie tells Liam he's brilliant and says goodbye. She tells me that one of his friends has a recording studio and he and his band recorded the single there that morning and dropped it straight off to the Shrubberylands FM studio – for a laugh, Liam says. He also says that copies can be made, if anyone wants to buy them, and the money can go to the sea life centre.

'We could sell Liam's CD at Dolphin Day!' Evie exclaims, excitedly. 'Perhaps it will make enough money to really help the sea life centre – perhaps it's not doomed after all!'

I grin a little nervously. But I agree that the CD is great and that it will be fantastic to play it and hopefully sell copies at Dolphin Day.

'It's really cool!' I say. 'Aisha's going to be thrilled! I wonder if she's heard it?' I text her to find out, while Evie goes to send emails to all our friends to tell them the exciting news.

This is certainly a dolphin dream come true!

Eco-info

Plastic from the UK is affecting the build up of plastic pollution in the world's oceans. Just because you can't see an immediate effect around you, doesn't mean that one isn't happening somewhere else. 80% of the rubbish in the plastic vortex in the Pacific Ocean comes from land, and only 20% from ships at sea.

Chapter Seven

'So bring your family and friends and come along to Dolphin Day! Gates open at two p.m. this afternoon, and all proceeds will go to help dolphins, turtles and other sea creatures,' announces Dave Groover on Shrubberylands FM. Liam had asked him if he would come to the event, after he'd played his CD on the radio and he'd agreed.

Dave Groover's been brilliant at supporting us – partly thanks to him mentioning it, the sponsored litter-pick last Sunday was a great success and people collected a huge amount of rubbish and sponsorship money. Hopefully we have now cleared the town of plastic bags! Nearly five hundred pounds was raised for the sea life centre. Evie and I are feeling a little more hopeful – and we are excited about Dolphin

Day, especially now that it's actually here. But so much needs doing at the sea life centre – we are still worried that we won't raise enough money to really help. Perhaps it will even be closed down . . . Evie alternates between giving me excited hugs and collapsing on a chair in despair with her head in her hands. I'm not sure how much more of this I can stand! I tend to despair more quietly that Evie – however at the moment I just feel nervous, but excited. I really want Dolphin Day to be the biggest success *ever*.

We head over to school at lunchtime to see how everything is going. Shrubberylands FM is playing over the sound system as everyone makes final preparations for Dolphin Day. Evie and I help Cassia and Ellen to set up the dolphin cake stall.

'I love the dolphin-shaped biscuits!' exclaims Evie enthusiastically. Each one has a little smiling dolphin face iced onto it. I make a mental note to buy Evie a dolphin biscuit if she starts despairing again any time soon.

A light breeze blows the bunting which has been hung everywhere. Some of the stalls are outside in the courtyard, others are in the school fields – thankfully it is a dry, bright day. The raffle stall in particular looks amazing, with lots of good prizes on display.

Soon the gates open and people flood in. Evie and I both feel overwhelmed at the level of support for Dolphin Day – I feel very proud. Evie jumps up and down with excitement, clapping her hands. I don't think she'll be having any more of her despairing fits for a while, which is a relief.

Dave Groover plays Liam's single, 'Dolphin Dream', repeatedly during the afternoon, and I notice Aisha wandering around dreamily, a happy smile on her face, listening to her poem. Her friends crowd around her excitedly, giggling.

Mr Woodsage makes an announcement to say that copies of the single are available for sale and anyone who would like to buy one should go to see him. I am thrilled to see more and more people approaching him during the course of the afternoon.

Evie and I are in charge of the tombola, which is next to Meltonio's ice-cream van. There is a queue of people buying ice-cream all afternoon – Evie and I have a Triple Chocolate Superscoop each. Everyone seems to be enjoying themselves, and there's a good, fun feeling to the event. Maybe it *will* all be enough to make a real difference . . .

'I want people to buy everything!' Evie says as she sells tombola tickets for the last few tombola prizes. 'Come on, people! Splash your cash! Do It for the Dolphins!'

'And for the sea life centre!' I yell. This is not a time to hold back. I want people to spend, spend, *spend*!

At the end of the afternoon, we help to draw the raffle tickets.

Mr and Mrs Plunkett and a sulky-looking Amelia are at the front of the crowd, standing hopefully with their raffle tickets, but they don't win anything.

Evie and I have a handful of raffle tickets between us, but fail to win anything either. Neither of us really cares about this – all we want is to save the sea life centre. The winners are thrilled with their prizes, and it's great to see people smiling so much all around us. After the raffle, Mr Woodsage makes a short speech, thanking everyone for coming and then he hands the microphone over to Todd, who's come along with Kate.

'I wonder what Todd's going to say?' I ask Kate, who's standing next to me.

Then he starts. 'On behalf of everyone here, I would like to thank two very special young ladies – Evie Evans and Lola Woodhouse.' He beckons to us and, smiling nervously, we step forward to join him. 'It was their idea to have a Dolphin Day, so I think that we should all give them a round of applause!' Everyone claps and cheers – Lee whoops loudly – and I feel myself going bright red. But I feel very *very* happy!

'Evie and Lola introduced me to the sea life centre a short while ago. We went to visit it a couple of weeks back and I've been there a few times since.'

Evie and I look at each other in surprise.

'I've been discussing things with the owners,' Todd continues, 'and I am going to take over running the sea life centre.'

'Oh, WOW!' Evie exclaims, clapping her hand to her mouth.

Todd grins at her and continues. 'I intend to run it on similar lines to my aquarium in Florida. More and more dolphins are becoming stranded along the coast of the UK and I'm hoping to build an ocean pool where stranded dolphins and other sea creatures can be nursed back to health before being released into the wild. By improving facilities too, we should be able to boost visitor numbers, and I also hope to raise money – and extend interest in marine conservation – by arranging dolphin watches and perhaps even swimming with wild dolphins.'

My jaw has dropped and Evie looks equally amazed. It is such a wonderful result! A dolphin disaster has, in an instant, been transformed into a dolphin dream – but it's *real*!

'And this is all thanks to Lola and Evie. Without them, it would never have happened!' Todd says in conclusion, turning to us and applauding.

The crowd applauds and cheers again, and Evie and I shriek and jump up and down before giving each other the biggest hug ever!

'Do I get a hug, too?' Todd McHenry asks.

'Of course! Oh, thank you! Thank you! Thank you!' Evie and I hug Todd, and Kate as well.

'I'd like to thank you, too,' says Todd. 'So I wondered if you two girls would like to come along with Kate and me tomorrow to try and see some wild dolphins. I can't promise that we'll see any, of course, but we've hired a boat and —'

'Oh – *yes please!*' Evie and I chorus, before Todd can finish his sentence.

The *Shrubberylands Sentinel*'s photographer, who has come to Dolphin Day with Wanda – a friend of Mum's and a journalist for the local paper – takes photos of Evie and me with Todd and Kate.

Dolphin Day has been a huge success!

Eco-info

More than a million seabirds and 100,000 marine mammals are estimated to be killed annually by plastic in the seas, and at least 250 different types of creatures have eaten or been entangled in the waste.

Chapter Eight

'Of course, the chance of seeing dolphins is not very high at the moment,' says Todd as he chokes the boat's engine into life. 'But the Burlingtons thought they saw a pod of dolphins on the coast yesterday.'

Evie and I exchange excited glances before training our binoculars on the horizon as the boat slowly chugs out to sea. It was a long journey to get here, but it is a calm clear day, and the sun is shining, so our spirits are high, although we are all wearing coats and life jackets against the cold breeze and sea spray.

Small waves sparkle and dance around the boat as the distance between us and the shore lengthens.

After a while Todd stops the engine and the boat bobs on the water, waves slopping gently against the sides.

'Keep looking!' says Kate, encouragingly, getting out a flask of hot tea and a packet of biscuits from her backpack.

'If we're really lucky, we could see a spot of team fishing,' says Kate. 'Dolphins like to form a line and herd the fish towards the shore. Then they pick them off one by one.'

'That's clever,' says Evie, scanning the waves for sleek grey shapes.

'Mostly at dawn and dusk,' says Todd. 'But I guess we could get lucky. Let's go a bit further out.' He chokes the outboard motor back into life and we search a different area.

I raise my binoculars and scan the sea for the dolphins' grey submarine shapes playing among the white spray made by the boat, or leaping out of the water ahead of us. I can imagine them so clearly – but will we actually get to see any real dolphins? My heart is beating madly in excitement as I search the waves for their fins or signs of them spouting.

'Slow down, Todd!' says Kate, suddenly. 'I can see one – two – three!'

Todd shuts down the engine and lets the boat drift.

We don't see anything for a few moments, but then Evie points, and I can see fins rising and disappearing across the surface of the water. We can't believe it – it looks like the dolphins are heading towards us!

The sleek grey shapes rise closer to the surface, coming to investigate the boat. Evie and I can see what look like shadows moving through the waves, twisting this way and that. Now, there are four of them, only a few metres away, and I can make out their fins and the strong up and down movement of their tails. My heart is beating fast – I have never felt so thrilled. Evie has covered her mouth with her hand so that she doesn't scream and scare them!

One of the dolphins then pokes his head up out of the water right by the hull of the boat, and I hold my breath. It makes gentle creaking noises, while the other dolphins swim under the boat, then rise to the surface in a shower of sea spray.

'That is *sooo* incredible!' sighs Evie. We are both transfixed by the beautiful sight.

'Dolphins often hunt fish at night, so they are usually pretty sleepy in the morning – you girls are really lucky to see them so active,' Todd tells us. He makes a sort of rapid clicking noise with his tongue and some of the dolphins chatter back.

'What are they saying?' I ask.

'They're thanking you for saving the sea life centre

so it can become a sanctuary for any of their friends who get injured or need help before they're returned to the wild,' Todd replies.

Evie and I laugh and take photos of the dolphins on our phones – I am going to text photos to our friends, who all want to know whether we have seen any dolphins yet. They are going to be so envious of our good luck – I wish I could share this experience with all of them.

After a while the dolphins lose interest in us and swim away, and we return to shore, thanking Todd and Kate profusely for our wonderful experience.

'I will *never* forget today!' Evie says. She has an ecstatic smile on her face all the way home. And I do too!

At school the next day, we are besieged by people wanting to know all about our dolphin watch and we tell them in great detail, falling over our words as we are still so excited about it.

We are right in the middle of double maths, when the head teacher comes into our class to tell us to come to her office. Evie and I are a bit worried about what we've done wrong. When we reach the office, we see there is a man in the room – it is Keith

Norris, manager of Kwikspend. Oh no! Surely he hasn't come to complain about our protest – that was ages ago! But when we go in, he stands up and shakes our hands.

'You showed me how strongly you felt about the world when you came to Kwikspend to protest about the number of plastic bags my store has been handing out. I read in the newspaper about your struggle to keep the sea life centre open, and about Dolphin Day. I love dolphins and was horrified to hear that plastic bags can be responsible for killing such beautiful creatures.'

Then he announces that Kwikspend is taking steps to be more eco-friendly in its day-to-day running and he feels that the time has come to stop handing out plastic bags in his store.

'Oh – cool!' I exclaim, and turn to Evie, whose eyes are shining with happiness. 'That is so . . . oh . . . it's so . . .' I am lost for words. Instead, I rush over and give Keith Norris a big hug. He looks very surprised. Even Evie looks taken aback. But I can see that she's overjoyed at the good news. This is a major eco-worrier triumph – the sort that should surely have been heralded by a fanfare of trumpets at the very least! But, with or without trumpets, I am totally thrilled!

* * *

'Well,' I say to Evie later that evening as we relax in her room with two raspberry smoothies. We haven't stopped smiling all day – first reliving the dolphin encounter with our friends, and then the good news about Kwikspend. 'We've achieved so much, when we thought everything was going wrong,' I continue. 'Plus, now people have realised how ungreen habits affect the things they love, we've ended up enthusing everybody again about green issues.'

'And we've saved the sea life centre,' Evie says.

'Not only saved it – improved it!' I add.

'And got plastic bags banned from Kwikspend!' Evie says.

'And that's because we never give up!'

'No – never!'

'Because . . .'

'We're ECO-WORRIERS!'

Eco-info

Never think that what you are doing isn't enough. By taking a small action to help the environment, you might be having a bigger effect than you think – other people can be inspired by your actions. If lots of people make even only small changes, that means a big difference could be made.

Go for it!

ECO-WORRIERS

Penguin Problems

Committed eco-worriers, Evie and Lola, are very, very concerned about green issues much to the irritation of their gas-guzzling families!

So when they find a penguin chick in the garden they're really worried. Have the ice caps finally melted and the poor penguins been forced into new lands?

It turns out that this particular penguin was taken from the local wildlife park. Could the penguin-napping be linked to the awful, but completely unfounded, rumours circulating about the park? Lola and Evie are determined to investigate further, and the more they find out the more suspicious they become . . .

ECO-WORRIERS

Tree Trouble

Lola and Evie are very concerned about the state of the planet and are determined to get their school to go green.

When they learn about the destruction of the tropical rainforests, they are even more concerned. What will happen to all those poor creatures who live in the trees – let alone the effect on climate change?

They decide to do their bit to help and organise a talent show, GreEntertainers, to raise money for TreeAid. But first they need to find some talent . . .

ECO-WORRIERS

Saving the Bacon

Lola and Evie have decided to become
vegetarian and eat only healthy,
locally sourced organic produce
and waste as little as possible.

They want everyone else to do the same
so they're delighted that their friend,
Meltonio, feeds all his leftovers to his
new pig, Samson. But then the girls
discover that Meltonio is fattening
Samson up for his Christmas dinner!
They must do something
to save the bacon!

For everything Eco-Worriers . . .

www.piccadillypress.co.uk/ ecoworriers

Check it out for:

Quizzes

Eco- facts

Downloads

Green ideas

New releases

Ways to get involved

More Eco-Worriers information than you can shake a tree at!